SISTERS OF ETERNAL BLISS

SISTERS OF ETERNAL BLISS
RISE OF THE GRANDMASTER™ BOOK THIRTEEN

BRADFORD BATES
MICHAEL ANDERLE

DISRUPTIVE IMAGINATION

This book is a work of fiction. All of the characters, organizations, and events portrayed in this novel are either products of the author's imagination or are used fictitiously. Sometimes both.

Copyright © 2022 by LMBPN Publishing
Cover Art by Jake @ J Caleb Design
http://jcalebdesign.com / jcalebdesign@gmail.com
Cover copyright © LMBPN Publishing
A Michael Anderle Production

LMBPN Publishing supports the right to free expression and the value of copyright. The purpose of copyright is to encourage writers and artists to produce the creative works that enrich our culture.

The distribution of this book without permission is a theft of the author's intellectual property. If you would like permission to use material from the book (other than for review purposes), please contact support@lmbpn.com. Thank you for your support of the author's rights.

LMBPN Publishing
PMB 196, 2540 South Maryland Pkwy
Las Vegas, NV 89109

Version 1.00, November 2022
eBook ISBN: 979-8-88878-012-1
Print ISBN: 979-8-88878-013-8

Previously published as part of the megabook *The Battle for the Kingdom*.

SISTERS OF ETERNAL BLISS TEAM

Thanks to our beta readers
Kelly O'Donnell, Larry Omans, Rachel Beckford

Thanks to the JIT Readers

Diane L. Smith
Veronica Stephan-Miller
Dorothy Lloyd
Angel LaVey
Dave Hicks

Editor
The Skyhunter Editing Team

LIST OF TIM'S CURRENT STATS AND SKILLS

"Tim" level twenty-two Hex Witch
Primary Stats
Strength: 17
Endurance: 34
Dexterity: 30
Intelligence: 62
Wisdom: 74
Perception: 6
Vitality: 4
Revitalization: 4
Luck: 7

Notable Gear
  Weapons
Simple Dagger of Dexterity, +1 (X2)
Greater Staff of Yin, +3 Endurance +7 Intelligence +7 Wisdom, Special effect: from light to darkness. For ten seconds, all healing caused by doing damage will receive a ten percent boost. Can be used once per encounter.

Orb of Concentration, +5 Intelligence +4 Wisdom

Armor

Circlet of Divine Wisdom, +1 Endurance +3 Intelligence +5 Wisdom

Shoulder Guards of the Spotless Mind, +1 Intelligence +2 Wisdom +1 to Perception, Vitality, Revitalization, and Luck. Special ability: Clarity. Removes any mind-altering effects instantly. Can be used once per day.

Hex Witch's Armament, +2 Endurance,+2 Dexterity +6 Intelligence +8 Wisdom, bonus to defense when standing within fifteen feet of the target or targets of your stance.

Dragon Hyde Jerkin, +2 to all base stats +1 to all secondary stats

Bearhide Wrist Guards of the Faithful, +1 Endurance +1 Wisdom, Special ability: Bear Necessities

Paul's Gloves of Mending, +7 Intelligence +4 Wisdom

Belt of Divine Inspiration, +1 Endurance +2 Intelligence +4 Wisdom

No That's Not a Brown Spot Leather Pants, +3 Endurance +2 Dexterity +4 Intelligence +3 Wisdom, Special ability: Flee

Arlen's Boots of Chaotic Intent, +3 Endurance +4 Intelligence +6 Wisdom, Special ability: Chaotic Intent. Any skill's effectiveness will be increased or decreased by one to ten percent.

Jewelry and Accessories

Arlen's Bracelet of Balance, +2 Endurance +4 Dexterity, Special ability to influence the outcome of Chaotic Intent

Wristband of the Faithful, +1 Endurance, ten seconds of double mana regeneration

Ring of Luminosity, +1 Endurance +2 Intelligence +3 Wisdom

Necklace of Hydration, +1 Endurance +2 Intelligence +5 Wisdom, Special ability: enhanced hydration

Trinket of the Smiling Monkey, +1 to a random stat

Skills

Hex of the Shattered Beast: Novice rank three
Appeal to the Goddess: Novice rank five
Curse of Sacrifice: Novice rank six
Night Vision: Apprentice rank one
Backstab: Apprentice rank four
Rectify: Apprentice rank four
Throwing Knives: Apprentice rank four
Disturbance: Apprentice rank five
Quick Feet: Apprentice rank five
Shadow Master: Apprentice rank six
Sneak: Apprentice rank six
Small Blades: Journeyman rank one
Snare: Journeyman rank one
Dodge: Journeyman rank six
Flame Burst: Journeyman rank six
Behold My Power: Journeyman rank seven
Who Needs a Shield: Journeyman rank seven
Divine Light: Journeyman rank eight
Healing Storm: Journeyman rank eight
Curse of Giving: Master rank one
Cleanse: Master rank one
Healing Orb: Master rank three

Stances

Way of the River
Way of the Boulder

Buffs

Weaken Undead: Journeyman rank two

Armor of Eternia: Journeyman rank seven
Attacks of the Faithful: Journeyman rank seven

Open Quests
The Stone of Immoratis

CHAPTER ONE

"Put your back into it, you lazy bastard!" Ironbeard shouted with glee as he pounded his magical hammer against the molten metal.

Tim adjusted his back against the seat and used his legs to work the massive bellows like a rowing machine. "This was supposed to be my vacation."

"You don't get to go have fun until we finish this. That was the deal." Ironbeard didn't look away from his work as small blasts of magical energy fizzled from his hammer into the breastplate he was creating.

Fucking dwarves and their deals.

When Ironbeard sat Tim down to offer him a leg up in his crafting education, he thought his teacher was magnanimous. The thought of gaining years' worth of knowledge for a few hours of work seemed too good to pass up. He quickly learned how much work the dwarf could fit in a day.

It wasn't until hour four, when his legs and back started to burn, that Tim offered Ironbeard bribes to quit early. Piles of gold, magical items, a discount at his trading kiosk—none of it was enough to make the dwarf reconsider their deal. Now the dwarf rebuked each of his offers by berating the state of his current staff and the refrain that good help was hard to find.

Tim was kicking himself for not trying to dicker on the price. He was so used to paying the listed cost for things that he never thought about bartering. In some cultures, every purchase was a negotiation, almost like a battle with a winner and a loser. Once he'd put his ass in the chair, Tim might as well have signed a contract that an army of corporate lawyers couldn't contest.

Now his lower back wanted a vacation.

As much as he liked bitching about the work, the tradeoff was worth it. When the voice in his head screamed for him to quit, saying that giving his word wasn't worth all this trouble, he kept his butt in the seat and worked the bellows like a champion. The longer he stayed inside *The Etheric Coast*, the more it reminded him of the responsibility of honoring a promise. He'd given his word to help until they completed the breastplate, so that was what he would do.

As soon as they finished, he would drown himself in icecold beer.

"I wish you'd told me the armor was for the fattest man in the entire fucking kingdom." Tim laughed but had to stop when it made breathing too hard.

Ironbeard roared with a deep belly laugh, and the sparks flying from each blast of his hammer changed color. "That was sloppy negotiating, boy. Always ask about the size of the client when it affects labor and material costs."

Wasn't that the truth?

Gritting his teeth against the cramps in his calves, Tim continued working the bellows. At this point, watching Ironbeard work was the only thing keeping him going. There was something to be said about Old World crafts and how lovingly people made them. A person certainly appreciated something as simple as a horseshoe a lot more when each one had to be shaped by hand. The magical suit of armor they were crafting was damn near priceless.

When it came right down to it, cramping legs were a small price to pay for achieving greatness.

Even Ironbeard's legendary stamina was fading. The time between each strike of his mighty hammer grew farther and farther apart. Slowly, a song started deep in the dwarf's throat and flowed out over the armor, adding its magic to the piece. His arm moved up and down, but a tremor built in the movements.

The longer Tim watched the smith work, the more he felt like he got the better side of the deal. Learning a new skill was priceless, but there was no way he could've swung the hammer with the dwarf's brutal efficacy. One thing was certain. If Tim ever wanted to be as good as Ironbeard, he would have to work on his strength and stamina.

Maybe he could buy some magical accessories to boost those stats while crafting. The one nice thing for him was that by adventuring as much as he did, he didn't have time to spend his hard-earned money and had plenty to burn on frivolous purchases. Tim pulled up the auction house menu on his user interface and ordered two rings and a necklace. Searching for the best deal helped him forget what he was doing as his legs kept pumping.

With a cry of triumph, Ironbeard tossed his hammer to the side and pulled the armor free to quench it before tempering it a final time. "I should've charged him more money."

Tim climbed down from the bellows and made it three steps before his legs turned to jelly. "I don't think I can walk. I guess the floor will be fine."

Maybe if I tip Grant enough, he'll carry me to the carriage.

"You're not staying here. I have plans." Ironbeard reached inside his leather vest and pulled out a flask. "Take a swig of this. It will put some hair on your balls."

"I'd like to believe the amount of testicle hair I have is just right." Tim took the proffered flask, hoping the liquid inside had other benefits besides rapidly growing testicular hair.

With one last lingering look at the dwarf, Tim tried to convince himself the flask contained a magical elixir. With his decision made, he unscrewed the cap and sipped. The warm cinnamon-flavored liquor roared down his throat and exploded with a splash of fire deep in his belly. Life crept back into his legs and lower back, and within a few moments, he was able to struggle to his feet with all the grace of a newborn calf.

Tim sipped again to speed up his recovery and handed the flask to Ironbeard. "What is that stuff?"

Buzzing with energy, Tim jumped up and down. He felt like he could run a marathon. Man, if this stuff was available back in college, he could've studied for days or maybe earned those abs. Ordering the Ab Blaster off late-night TV was about as far as he ever made it, but with this kind of juice, he could do sit-ups until the sun came up.

If Red Bull gives you wings, this shit will send you to the moon.

Ironbeard tucked the flask away. "Stamina potion. Costs a pretty penny, but when you have deadlines, things have to get done. Sometimes sleeping is a luxury I can't afford."

"I'm the exact opposite. I could give up work to spend the rest of my days in bed with ShadowLily in an instant." Tim clapped the dwarf on the back as they headed toward the door. "Hey, I've been meaning to ask, is there a Mrs. Ironbeard?"

Ironbeard grumbled. "There won't be if I don't get out of here soon. Dotie has a thing about punctuality. If I'm not on time, I don't get to punch in."

"Well, don't let me keep you." Tim stepped out of the shop, and the door slammed so fast the wind pushed him forward a step. "Guess he wasn't kidding."

Tim did a quick clothes swap. This time it was more to get out of the smelly items he was wearing than trying to throw off any enemy pursuers, but it never hurt to be careful. It wasn't long ago he'd used this very market to avoid the man with the orange sash. Switching from one outfit to another almost instantly made it hard for anyone to track him in the crowded marketplace.

I'm like Jason Bourne. You never know I'm coming.

Not that he'd have to worry now. They were friends with royalty, for fuck's sake. Anyone who wanted to mess with them should've done it before the king was on their speed dial. Now screwing with the Blue Dagger Society could have significant consequences. It was the kind of security you couldn't buy and should've been absolute, but dancing close to greatness could put a target on a person's back as easily as it rained riches upon their heads.

The Blue Daggers had enough powerful enemies. The dark goddess Vitaria would no doubt put more in their path as Eternia finished powering up. He doubted their trip back to the desert would be as easy as hopping a few portals. They would have to fight for it like they always did.

Fighting was fine with Tim. Entering a dungeon meant new encounters and mechanics, along with better loot. He had two pieces of Arlen's gear, but he wanted more. Getting a cool set this early in the game might carry him for quite some time. It would be nice not having to worry about upgrades for a bit, but then again, upgrades kept him coming back for more action.

With the day's work completed, the only action he was looking for was the loving arms of his woman.

The inn was too close for him to call for a ride, so he walked. The evening air was crisp with a hint of salt in the breeze rolling in from the ocean. People packed the streets tonight, and the foot traffic didn't die on the way to the slums like it used to. In fact, it probably wasn't even fair to call it the slums anymore. It was amazing what hard work and a few thousand gold coins could accomplish.

The best part was everyone who'd lived in the area before was still there. It was revitalization with a heart. Some of the best messages he'd received were from people whose businesses were thriving because of the trading kiosk at the inn and the newly cobbled roads. It was a lot easier to get a cart through the wet streets of the slums on cobbles than it was in the mud.

The city of Promethia was thriving with all of the new businesses created by the players, but no other restaurant was as busy as Joe's. The man simply had food that no one else could make. Now that the famous chef enlisted Roberto, people couldn't stop raving about the new items. If patrons came to eat, surely they would stop and take care of their shopping before leaving. Whenever someone purchased at his kiosk, Tim used the money to further his construction projects.

Joe's had a line outside as usual, and the healing shack was closed for the evening. The Blue Dagger Inn's front doors were thrown wide open, and people had packed inside.

"What in the hell is going on?" Tim pushed through the crowd.

A hand clamped down on his wrist.

"Follow me," Liz growled as she tugged Tim toward the bar.

Letting himself be carried along in her wake, Tim wondered if something was wrong. "Why are all these people here?"

"Because your idiot tank decided to throw a karaoke party," Liz growled. "Do you know what I've had to endure for the last three hours?"

Tim laughed. "Let me tell you a story about a rowboat."

"Fuck off. You're tending bar until this shit is over." Liz dragged Tim around the corner and slapped an empty mug in his hand. "Get to pouring. We have thirty thirsty people waiting for drinks out there."

Tim watched as Liz left to join Ernie in the kitchen. When

he looked up, the waitresses were all staring at him. "So, beers it is then."

Working behind the bar wasn't rocket science when he didn't have to mix drinks. Any idiot could fill a mug or pitcher with delicious beer. All he had to do was keep them flowing. Mug, pitcher, mug, pitcher… As soon as he set them down, one of the waitresses carried them away. Someone started to sing, and they weren't that bad.

An hour later, Tim understood why Liz bailed.

Cassie strolled up to the bar, weaving gently back and forth. "Isn't this great?"

"This is fucking great!" ShadowLily roared as though her friend hadn't spoken.

Tim looked at the two women sauced to the gills and grinned. "Where's JaKob?"

"Head in a book." ShadowLily swayed a little to the newest song.

Cassie grunted. "That's about the only place he'll get to put his head tonight."

"So he's at the library, and you threw a party." Tim looked at the two women as they giggled.

"That sums it up." ShadowLily yanked on Tim's hand. "Come on, do a song with us."

They could barely walk, and he could barely sing. This was going to be a disaster.

A man walked out on a small, raised platform. "Please welcome to the stage, Kevin McGrath."

"Oh fuck!" Cassie ducked.

ShadowLily motioned for Tim to duck. "You should get down."

"Why? It's just some guy. I've been slinging beers for an hour already. No one is that bad." Tim looked from his girlfriend to the tank.

Cassie groaned. "Might as well sober us up. The party is about to be over."

"It can't be that bad." Tim looked at the stage. "Let's go, Kevin!" He clapped.

The man walking out on stage was wearing a dress, and his look was fierce. Tim didn't know much about drag queens, but he'd seen an episode or two of *Dragnificent* and thought they were bloody brilliant. At least those four ladies were. He'd have been happy to call any of them friends.

Kevin strutted up and down the stage as the music played. "Start spreading the news…"

"She's not so bad." Tim looked at the stage and back at the two women before returning to pour beers.

Cassie slumped. "Wait for it."

ShadowLily cringed. "Liz is going to kill us."

"Promethia, Promethia!" Kevin screeched. "I don't sleep. I'm the king of this heap!"

Glass mugs flew at the stage, and Tim watched in awe as Kevin dodged them all and kept singing. "He's good."

Cassie scowled.

"At dodging stuff, not at singing." Tim jumped up on the bar. "Those mugs cost money, you ungrateful pricks. The next person I see throwing one is going to be sober in an instant."

A man sailed a mug straight at Kevin's head as he pirouetted across the stage. Tim's Cleanse spell hit him a moment later, and the man looked down at his hands and back at Tim.

"What did you do to me?" He stared at his outstretched hands as if they belonged to someone else.

Tim laughed and put a fresh mug of beer in the man's hand. "This will start setting things right, but no more throwing mugs."

"Don't fuck with this one, boyos. I'm as sober as a frog on Sundays." The man drank half his mug in a gulp, and his friends cheered.

The mood in the bar quieted down a bit after that, and Liz returned. "Thanks for the breather."

ShadowLily grabbed Tim by the belt. "Why don't we go up upstairs so I can make a man outta you?"

"I'd sober you up, but I'm kinda liking DrunkenLily." Tim didn't need to be yanked toward the stairs more than once.

"Liz, the bar is yours," Tim called as he chased his girlfriend up the stairs.

Tonight was going to be a good night.

God, he loved vacation!

CHAPTER TWO

"Is that him?" Liam hissed.

Klever squinted into the darkness. "I think so."

"You think so. You damn well better be sure." Liam motioned to his men to be ready.

"Ain't ever seen more than a picture of the man, but I'd wager that's him." Klever squinted again and nodded. "I'm sure of it."

Liam clapped him on the back. "I hope so. Duke Ravenstorm isn't known for her forgiveness."

Klever gulped, and Liam smiled as he walked back to the group of thugs. His mother's name wasn't good for a lot, but it always inspired fear. Fear was a healthy motivator for some men, and Liam used it when needed. It was also good to remind the man that shit rolled downhill, and he wouldn't hesitate to throw him under the bus if this plan went sideways.

His band of thugs spread out and encircled the man before he knew what was going on. There was a frightened squawk, and the fists fell. The poor guy didn't stand a chance when it was ten on one. The only good news for their target was they weren't there to kill him.

Mother only wanted a word.

Liam moved toward the circle, and the men parted, revealing the crumpled form of a man lying on the cobbles. Running to his side, Klever flipped the body over and looked at his face. He turned back toward his boss, and his face was full of terror.

"It's not him." Klever started to shake.

This wasn't good.

Mother didn't handle incompetence well, and it wasn't only the bumbling idiot who would pay for it. She wouldn't torture him, but there were plenty of ways to make a man suffer, and his mother knew them all. What a pretty pickle he was in now.

There was only one way out of it.

"I'm sorry, old friend." Liam drew his sword.

Torchlight filled the mouth of the alley. "What's going on here?"

"Just one time, I'd like something to go my way." He turned to face the man with the torch and pointed his sword at him. "Grab him."

Instead of turning to run as Liam expected, the man pulled his sword free and tossed his torch to the side.

"By order of the crown, I command you to throw down your weapon and come with me." The lone warrior sounded in complete command despite the disadvantage in numbers.

Liam snarled at his men, "I didn't say to stop."

"As commander of the watch, I order you to stop this moment." Brennen lifted his sword prepared to go down swinging.

Klever moved to stand next to Liam. "That's him."

"Helps when they announce themselves, doesn't it?" Liam slipped his sword into its sheath and clapped his friend on the back.

I would've hated to kill him.

Wiping the rain from his eyes, Klever smiled. "Indeed it does."

Two of his men went down before Brennen was overwhelmed by the rest. It didn't take long for them to finish binding the man. As soon as he was tied up and gagged, Liam whistled, and a man rode toward them with two horses in tow. His men tossed the watch commander over one of the horses and held out the reins of the other.

"I can't promise this will be pleasant for you, Commander, but it will be interesting." Liam turned toward his men. "Get the injured to the healer, and someone clean up this mess. We don't want the guard asking questions."

He didn't wait to see if they carried out his orders. He trusted that they were. Everyone who worked in the duke's service knew the price for failure and disobedience. She wasn't an easy woman, but she also showered her men with wealth the other nobles lorded for themselves. They loved her for it.

The king was weak, his wife was gone, and half of the kingdom hated the prince. The time was right for them to make a move. It had to be, or the duke never would've made a play as bold as this. If anyone knew it was them who attacked an officer of the crown, they would be labeled traitors. Despite their strength, they couldn't take on the entire kingdom. They needed allies.

Brennen would be one of theirs. He just didn't know it yet.

"I have a problem that I need your help with." Duke Ravenstorm turned the thumbscrews a little tighter.

Watch Commander Brennen's only answer was an almost silent whimper.

She liked that, the sound of a man in pain. What was it about having a cock that made a man think he was better than a woman? The things were only meat-tubes with dangly sacks attached. Ugh, and those sacks, how hairy and unattractive.

And just try asking a man to shave.

The duke almost laughed out loud at the absurdity of it. They all acted like their body hair was a gift from the goddess herself, but if a woman dared to have hair down there, better call in the guards to have her shaved on the spot. She was tired of their crap, her husband's crap. Still, she sat in his seat now while his body was food for the worms.

Sometimes she liked to visit his grave to gloat.

Men also served a purpose like her son Liam. He was a loyal soldier, but he would also be the one to secure their legacy. That was what she was trying to do right now. Looking down at the watch commander, she tightened the thumbscrews one more time.

Merely to hear the delicious sound of his whimpers.

"I hoped we could see eye-to-eye on this matter," Duke Ravenstorm purred. "There's still time to change your mind."

Brennen looked up, his eyes blazing with hatred. "I would rather die than let your men into the marquess' castle. Your limp-dick son doesn't deserve a title."

"Maybe you would be more malleable if I were to put the screws to your sister instead." Ravenstorm smiled sweetly. "I'm sure my son would be willing to give her work as a concubine after your death."

Brennen surged forward. "You keep your limp-dick son away from my sister!"

It always came down to dicks.

Letting out a slow sigh, Ravenstorm signaled to her assistant, and he placed the clamp in her hand. "I've often wondered how flat a penis can become."

She held up the clamp and snapped it shut for dramatic effect.

"You don't have the guts to kill me. When the marquess

hears of this, he'll..." Brennen's sentence trailed off. He knew the inflated old windbag would never do anything to help him.

Reaching out, she grabbed the insolent fucker's jaw in her hands. "He'll what? Come for you?" She pushed Brennen back with disgust. "You overestimate the man."

Brennen's eyes fell. "Then do your worst, but I'll never help you sack the kingdom."

"It's a shame you're on the wrong side of this fight. I so rarely run into men of honor. Part of me finds it sad that it's my obligation to deprive the world of such rarity." Ravenstorm set the clamp down and pulled out her dagger.

There was no fear in the watch commander's eyes as she plunged the dagger into his stomach, only defiance. A few more pokes and the defiance turned to fear. She liked that a lot better. She wasn't lying when she said that his honor was rare among her acquaintances, but she had hope that her second meeting of the evening would go much more smoothly. With one final look at the watch commander as he choked and burbled, she slid her dagger home and strode for the door.

Maybe his sister would be the key to unlocking his tongue? The most emotion the fool showed the entire night was when she'd mentioned the woman. Love could be a useful emotion, and it was the easiest one to exploit after all. People would do all kinds of stupid things for love, but they would do almost anything to save someone they cared about.

She could use that, and she would.

Misha was by her side in a second. "Might I suggest a change of clothes before your next appointment?"

Duke Ravenstorm looked down at her dress. "Shit, I just bought this. Get the healer in here. I'm not done with him yet."

Her assistant *tsked*. "I told you to wear the smock." She pointed at a new dress waiting in the corner of the room by the stairs.

"You knew I'd never listen and had new attire waiting." The

duke slipped out of her outfit and moved toward the clean one. "What would I ever do without you?"

Misha helped her into the dress. "Well, you certainly wouldn't look as presentable."

"I present to you, Lord Briarthorn and his wife, Lady Joscelin." The footman escorted the lord and his wife into the room.

Duke Ravenstorm rose to meet her guests. "It's an honor to have you at my table."

Lord Briarthorn bowed stiffly. "I assure you the honor is ours."

The duke motioned for her guests to sit, took her place at the head of the table, and poured a glass of wine. "I've heard you're a man who doesn't enjoy mincing words."

"You heard correctly, but I heard this was a meeting I couldn't afford to miss." Lord Briarthorn looked at her pointedly.

Laughing as if the joke was on them, the duke watched her guests over the rim of her glass. "Afford is a very apt word considering I've purchased all your debt."

"You've what?" Lord Briarthorn looked at her with panic etched across his features. "How is that possible?"

The duke set down her glass and stated matter of factly, "I begged, borrowed, killed, and fucked for it, but in the end, every single one of them was willing to sell you out for something.

"Now I own you." She motioned for her servants to bring the first course. "I'd like to offer you the chance to earn it all back. I only want one thing."

"Honey, what is she talking about?" Joscelin's fury was rising. "We don't have any debts."

Laughing again, the duke poured more wine. "Your

husband isn't nearly as good at gambling as he thinks, and your businesses are a domino away from collapsing.

"I'm the domino." Ravenstorm enjoyed the taste of a good red.

"What are your terms?" Lord Briarthorn was quivering.

Is that rage or fear?

"Your daughter marries my son. After their first male child is born, I'll return your assets in full." The duke leaned back and waited for their answer.

"And if we refuse?" Joscelin looked ready to march out of the room.

Eyeing the couple like a hungry predator, the duke replied without a trace of her previous good humor. "Then I hope you enjoy sleeping in the street because I own all of it, and I'll take it from you in a heartbeat."

"Then we'll start over." Joscelin stood and held her hand out for her husband.

"The hell we will." Lord Briarthorn smacked her hand away. "It's long overdue for Lucy to find a suitable match, and the duke's son would make as fine a husband as any."

Joscelin turned to leave. "Then make your deal, but do it knowing that Lucy will never forgive you for it."

"She will, and you must," Lord Briarthorn commanded, but his eyes never left the duke. "I accept your terms."

That wasn't nearly as hard as the duke imagined it would be. "You really should stay for dinner. The second course is divine." She couldn't resist twisting the knife.

Lord Briarthorn rose from his seat. "It seems my wife has grown ill. I do hope you'll excuse me as I attend to her."

"Of course, women do have such sensibilities." She motioned for him to go.

Desmond and the king were making alliances and moving against her, but the duke was making new friends too. This was it. She'd cast her dice when she'd joined Cronos in her mad plan to kill the king and secure the royal treasure trove of magical artifacts. The only thing she could do now was to wait and see how it all played out. If there was one thing they should know, it was that she wasn't a quitter, and she never lost no matter the cost.

When this was over, no one would ever forget her name.

CHAPTER THREE

It was never a good day when her parents stopped by, but when they showed up after nine in the evening, the news they carried with them must be truly disheartening.

The truth was, Lucy Briarthorn had outgrown her parents years ago. Her assets nearly rivaled theirs, and she was well on the way to passing them. Whenever her parents died, it would catapult her into the ranks of the elite. At least when it came to wealth and influence. She would make sure the other nobles knew she earned her place and that her parents hadn't handed it to her.

Reginald poked his head back into the study. "Your parents are waiting in the parlor. They look grim."

"Just what I need on top of everything else." Lady Briarthorn rose from her desk. "Let's find out what new pile of shit they've stepped into now."

Snorting, Reginald opened the door wider. "Surely, I don't know what you mean."

She nodded at him as she swept from the room. Reginald might feign innocence, but he was privy to her every secret and knew when to keep his mouth shut. He was more than a servant and a doorman. He was a bodyguard and confidant. When there was no one else she could trust in her life, there was good old dependable Reggie.

Her father scowled as she entered the parlor. "Did you intend to keep us waiting all night?"

"I intended to keep you waiting until I finished what I was working on." She sat without waiting to be told. "Now you have my full attention."

Her father looked damn near ready to burst.

"You should watch your tone," he growled but didn't say anything else when her mother placed a hand on his arm.

Lucy accepted a glass of wine from Reginald and motioned for him to leave without offering her parents refreshments. "This is my house, bought and paid for with my money. While you're in it, you will show me the respect I've earned, daughter or not."

She sipped her wine and waited for the fireworks.

Instead, it was her mother who spoke. "Lucy, we have a bit of a problem."

"How much did he lose this time?" She was tired of helping him hide his gambling.

"You know?" Her mother looked shocked.

Lucy gave a bitter snort. "Who do you think he comes to when no one else will lend him money?"

Joscelin Briarthorn dropped her husband's arm as if he were a leper. "You said she was repaying what you lent her. What a fool I've been."

"There's nothing for it now. You heard what the duke said," Henry snarled.

Lucy had about enough of this entire conversation. "What did the duke say?"

The words came out with more venom than she intended, but her parents had a way of putting her in a mood.

Joscelin let out a sob.

"You." Her father pointed at her as if she were nothing more than a prize to be bundled up and delivered to the highest bidder. "You're going to marry Liam Ravenstorm."

Lucy let out a scornful laugh. "I'd rather be dead."

"And see your parents tossed into the streets like filth?" Henry raged. "Of course, you would. You spiteful girl. All you ever care about is yourself."

Joscelin slapped him across the face so hard her husband fell out of his seat and hit the floor hard. "I've heard enough. You put us in this mess, and our daughter will not be on the hook for your mistakes."

She turned to face Lucy. "Or my willful ignorance."

"Mom, what's going on?" Lady Briarthorn wrapped her arms around her mother as she sobbed.

"He's lost it all, and that devil of a woman bought all his debts." She leaned back. "I'd rather sleep in the streets than sell off my daughter like cattle."

Lucy kept her eyes hard. "Oh, I don't think it will come to that."

"So you would let our family name fall to ruins?" Henry stared at his daughter with disbelief. "Let our history, our pride, be turned into ruins and mud?"

That was the final straw.

"When they look back on our history, you'll only be remembered as the man who failed at cards." Lucy downed her glass of wine. "I'll be remembered as the Briarthorn who made her fortune."

Henry nodded. "That may be so, but when the duke can't get what she wants the polite way, she'll get it by other means."

Not being able to pay one's debts got them locked up. If her father truly gambled everything away, it would take her entire fortune to repurchase it at a fair price. The duke wouldn't be fair. She might not feel any love for her father at the moment, but being bad at cards shouldn't force a man into a lifetime of hard manual labor.

Not that he had the muscles for it.

Knowing the duke's reputation, her parents probably wouldn't receive fair treatment either. Daily beatings or worse would be in store for them. If Ravenstorm got tired of playing with them, she'd probably have them killed outright. People died in the labor camps all the time. No one blinked an eye.

Was she really going to have to marry Liam?

For the first time in her life, Lucy felt utterly overwhelmed by the situation. This wasn't like her. When there was a problem, she twisted it into an advantage. That was how she conquered the business world, and that was what she needed to do now. The last thing she could do was accept this deal only to have her father throw it all away again six months from now.

"There will be terms." Lucy felt a little bile in the back of her throat at her father's triumphant smile.

He moved forward to embrace her. "I knew you'd see sense."

"Sense would be staying away from the cards." She pushed him off. "I'll have Reginald draw up papers. You'll transfer all of the family's holdings into my ownership, and you will have an allowance."

Henry sputtered. "The audacity."

Now that this was a simple matter of negotiation, Lucy felt much more like herself. "The choice is yours, daily beatings or worse by Ravenstorm's men, or you swallow your pride and take what I give you."

Joscelin looked between them, her heart breaking as the rift between the two of them grew to near-insurmountable levels. "This can't be our only option."

"It is, and he knows it." Lucy would've smirked if it wasn't her on the auction block. "The question is can he go through with it?"

Henry sat down heavily as if his legs had gone out. "Either way, I lose everything."

"That's not true. There is one way you keep my respect." Lucy knew he'd never take it.

Broken like someone had stolen his businesses from him instead of losing them in a game of cards, Henry met her eye. "The businesses are yours."

"Of course they are." Lucy stood. "I trust you can see yourselves out." She left.

Now that she was out of the room, her heart was racing. "Reginald, have the carriage brought around."

Gaston was wrestling a keg of beer behind the bar when the door to the inn blew open.

Lucy Briarthorn walked into the Blue Dagger, and he instantly knew something was wrong. He'd never seen her with a hair out of place, and now she was wet and shivering with makeup running down her cheeks.

He was over the bar in an instant, catching her lightly before her legs gave away. It felt like when she saw him all the life went out of her. What in the hell was happening? She had some terrible news, he could tell, but that couldn't be it. There was nothing the two of them couldn't overcome if they were together.

Lucy looked up at him through tearful eyes. "I'm getting married."

"Well then, I better make a dishonest woman out of you while I still have the chance." Gaston lifted her gently into his arms, trying to force a smile onto his face.

Things between them would've never worked out anyway.

The only time anyone mentioned a lady and an assassin in the same story was in a bawdy joke. They weren't a joke, not to him, and he thought she'd felt the same way. Nothing he could do about it now.

Sometimes you have to make the best of things.

Lucy let out a stifled laugh. "It seems the least I could do."

His heart skipped a beat. Then it started hammering. Something was stirring down below, but Gaston had to find out if she was serious or not. The last thing he wanted was to set her down and have her feel a little something poking her first. He was about to panic when he remembered she said yes, and that was why he was in this wonderfully wicked mess in the first place.

The fact of the matter was he loved her, and he'd never stop.

Gaston swept through the entrance to his rooms below the inn, slamming the door shut with a kick. He raced down the stairs before she could change her mind about their decision. A moment later, he was tossing her down on the bed like a sack of flour. Not the most romantic, but there was a hunger in her eyes that said hurry up and get on with it.

Ripping off his vest, Gaston fell upon her like a wolf, and together they howled into the night.

CHAPTER FOUR

Tim looked around the table, hungry for more than food. "So, does anyone have the four-one-one on what happened?"

"He must've been watching nineties movies again." Shadow-Lily rolled her eyes. "Not everyone knows there used to be a number you called for information."

Laughing as he took a bite of his pancakes, JaKobi shook his head. "It wasn't a psychic hotline."

There was a *thump* under the table, and Cassie grinned like a card shark about to take the entire pot. "Someone has to know something."

Liz poured each of them a full glass of rumpleberry juice. "I only heard the words, 'I'm getting married.' Then there was a lot of unintelligible grunting."

"You don't tell anyone about our sex noises, do you?" Tim blushed.

Liz grinned. "No, but you did."

A door opened. Every head snapped to the stairs leading down to Gaston's chambers, but that entry was still closed.

Almost as one with sighs of disappointment, they turned to see who was waiting at the inn's entrance.

"I thought after our last meeting I'd be entitled to a warmer reception." Prince Desmond beamed at the group of adventurers as he made his way toward the table.

Lorelei laughed at the prince's crestfallen expression. "It's not you. We were all waiting for...." Her voice trailed off as the door to Gaston's chambers opened.

Lady Briarthorn stepped out wearing a cute little riding outfit. Her normally pale cheeks had a rosy tinge, and while she looked happy, quiet desperation hid below the surface. She closed the door behind her and looked up to find every eye in the inn turned in her direction.

"They never told me the barn contained such a stud. I might have to negotiate further breeding privileges." Lucy tossed out the casual joke as she scanned the room.

When she saw Prince Desmond, her casual demeanor instantly became subservient.

Dropping smoothly to one knee, Lucy spoke. "Sorry for my crass demeanor, Highness. I didn't expect to see you here."

Motioning for her to rise, Desmond wore a quizzical expression as he looked around the inn. "Think nothing of it. These adventurers tend to have interesting effects upon us all."

Tim moved his plate to the next spot, making room for Lucy. "Would you care to join us for breakfast?"

"I couldn't possibly." Lady Briarthorn stared daggers at Tim as he tried to keep the smile from his face.

Desmond knew something was going on but not exactly what, so he used his princely powers to help get to the bottom of it. "Please do join us. I insist."

"Then I'd be delighted." Lucy curtsied to Desmond before sitting and giving Tim a not-so-secret finger signal.

She's never going to forgive me.

Gaston ran into the room shirtless, carrying a nice black riding jacket. "Lucy, you forgot your coat."

"Oh, this is delicious." The prince wasn't talking about the pancakes sitting in front of him. "Who's your friend, Lady Briarthorn?"

Handing the jacket to Lucy, Gaston turned and extended his hand. "Stop acting like we didn't play drinking games for five hours the other night."

Gaston rushed around the table with his arms open and pulled Desmond into a hug. Tim waited for the prince to squawk and push the assassin away, but he seemed equally happy to see the man. Whatever they bonded over happened after Tim had gone to bed, but clearly, the men were closer than an assassin and a prince should be.

Liz handed Gaston a shirt. "If you're going to go around hugging people, the least you could do is wear some clothes."

Gaston put on the shirt and rumpled Liz's hair like his little sister. She swatted his hand away in the same manner, and her look let him know there would be hell to pay when the company was gone. The burly man didn't care. He'd already turned his attention back to the prince.

"In fact, Lucy and I might have a problem you can help with." Gaston placed a hand on Lady Briarthorn's shoulder and gave it a gentle squeeze. "You see, the duke is forcing Lucy to marry Liam."

Lady Briarthorn pulled away in a sharp motion. "Forced might be putting it too boldly."

"The hell it is. That bitch bought up all her family's debt and is using it against them." He turned from Lucy's shocked face to Desmond's set in stone. "There has to be something we can do to stop it."

The prince thought about it for a moment, and his eyes lit up like he'd come up with a ridiculous plan. "Maybe there's something we can do."

Trying to keep her face serene but failing miserably, Lucy reached out and stroked Gaston's chest longingly. "We had this same conversation last night, but I'm resolved in my course of action."

Gaston stormed away. "Can't get married if I kill the little bastard first."

Bowing gracefully, Lucy locked eyes with the prince. "I'm sorry to excuse myself, Your Highness. I find that I have a lot to accomplish today and very little time in which to get it done."

"Of course, please do not let me detain you further." Prince Desmond looked more than happy to let her go and avoid the entire business.

JaKobi tossed his fork onto his plate. "Well, that was a fucking letdown. I wanted to have some fun. How often is it you get to mock nobility for doing the walk of shame?"

Groaning as he stretched his pants around the waist, the ember wizard leaned back. "Instead, we got hit over the head with the depression stick."

"Right to the face." ShadowLily winced as if remembering an old emotional wound.

Cassie didn't look too concerned about it. "Relax, guys, there has to be something we can hit to make this problem go away."

"We're still on vacation, right?" JaKobi didn't want to give up his newly found library privileges yet.

Tim laughed. "Not since Lorelei got back this morning. Eternia might need a day or two longer, but we're on the clock."

Turning toward the prince, Tim filled his glass of juice. "Any ideas?"

He didn't know much about politics, and royal politics even less, but if anyone could help Lucy get out of a marriage she didn't want to be in, it had to be the prince. What was the point of being in charge if you couldn't make an exception to the rules now and again? Tim's need to help his friends probably blinded him, but stopping a wedding couldn't be that hard.

Prince Desmond sipped his juice and set the glass down. "I think there might be something we can do for each other. I dislike the duke but putting an end to this will cost me. I need something from you first."

"Let me guess. You already have something in mind?" Cassie grunted.

Desmond smiled. "Indeed, I do. Now that my father is back, we've decided to start rooting out the conspirators who helped Cronos with her plan. We've found a location a little closer to home that we need to deal with."

Tim knew they'd be going back there eventually.

"The Sisters of Eternal Bliss have been allowed many freedoms, but today that ends." Desmond looked around the table. "Help me end their plague upon our citizens, and I will see that Lady Briarthorn never has to marry Liam."

Quest Received: Tit for Tat

Prince Desmond has come to you with the classic "you scratch my back, I'll scratch yours" situation. He wants you to dismantle the Sisters of Eternal Bliss so they can no longer feed upon the citizens of Promethia.

Reward: Desmond will stop the wedding of Liam to Lucy Briarthorn.

Tim hated taking quests that didn't have physical rewards, but Lucy and Gaston were his friends. He wouldn't let their chance at love die because her father screwed up. They deserved to be happy, and if he could help them stay that way he'd do everything in his power to assist.

He accepted the quest.

"I've been to the sisters' lands before. We won't last long without something to combat their magic." Tim wanted to make sure the prince knew this was no small task.

Prince Desmond finished a bite of his pancakes. "In that regard, I have something for you." He tossed Tim a scroll. "It's the recipe for a potion that should keep you safe."

"Should?" Cassie grumbled. "Might as well be a wet dollar bill in a knife fight."

JaKobi winked at her. "Babe, with you leading us, it might as well be a howitzer."

Lorelei snatched the scroll. "I'll get this to Ernie, and we'll test it out before we go inside."

"Of course." Tim smiled. "See if you can track down some rope."

The spirit archer gave him a quizzical look but nodded and headed out the door in search of their poison master.

Pushing his plate aside and standing, Prince Desmond also moved toward the door. "Thank you for breakfast, but I also have other matters to attend to."

Tim waited for the prince to leave before he looked at everyone at the table with a huge shit-eating grin. "I almost lost it when she called Gaston her stud."

"And with the prince sitting right there." JaKobi's eyes lit with amusement.

Lorelei came back into the room with a fresh mug of coffee for the table. "It's so sad, but we're going to make it better."

"Fuck yeah! No one should get married because it's good business." ShadowLily stood. "I don't know how long it'll take for Ernie to brew that potion, but if you have any pressing business you need to wrap up, now is the time."

Tim leaned back in his chair, looking content. "It's like you guys don't even need me anymore."

"If we're about to get busy again, I'm going to need you upstairs in five." ShadowLily grinned.

"That's a quest I'd be happy to accept." Tim ran for the stairs.

He didn't know what to expect when he woke up this morning, but extra sex and a brand-new quest was one of the best ways he'd ever started a day.

CHAPTER FIVE

Tim felt like he had one up on every hobbit that ever lived. Those cute little guys might get elevenses, but he was about to get a second breakfast after having his toes curled by the hottest half-elven mist slayer around. Tim didn't know if it was the pointy ears, rocking bod, wicked smarts, or that big ole heart that made him want to be with her, but he knew that he never wanted to let her go.

And he meant every word doubly when there was a second stack of pancakes and a gallon of coffee in his future.

He sent a quick message to Liz while ShadowLily finished her shower, then he climbed into the shower. It might've taken a good bit of magic and a fair bit of gold to get it installed and working, but it was worth it. Baths had grown on him a bit, but nothing beat the feel of a good warm shower. If he could sit in one for hours and think, the world might not have a single problem left.

Alas, his skin and the world's water table couldn't handle his shower needs.

While the hot water raced down his back, Tim pulled up his user interface. There were a few random messages in his inbox that he discarded without reading, and he found a letter from Mr. Applebottom. He wanted to let him know Watch Commander Brennen's sister was a model tenant, and she was doing good business. The note reminded him that she'd invited them to see her shop, and he needed to make an appearance.

Tim set a reminder using the interface and moved on to updating his skills. It had been a while since he looked them over, and now might be his only chance for a day or so. He pulled up the list, which was longer than he expected. The minor updates typically added a slight stat boost, so he decided to skip those and focus on the skills that moved up a tier in rank. He could look at his updated summary later to see the smaller boosts.

With the flick of a mental finger, he dismissed all the lesser updates and moved on to the good stuff.

Skill Increased: Hex of the Shattered Beast
Rank: Apprentice one
Good boy, good boy. No, we're not talking about your beast. We're talking about you. You've reached the apprentice ranks with your very loveable beast, and it's about to receive a new perk. While Hex of the Shattered Beast is active, the target of your beast will receive a five percent reduction in damage taken. See, a good dog is always learning new tricks.

Things were already off to an amazing start.

A grin spread across Tim's lips as he reread the update. Reducing damage taken was almost as good to a healer as increasing their healing done. Any less damage Cassie took meant he could contribute to the fight in other ways. It was nice not to stay pigeonholed in one role. Reduced damage allowed him to be flexible.

The next skill up was Appeal to the Goddess. It received a small buff, but he mostly skipped over it because when he could only use the skill every so often, it got shoved to the back of his thoughts. Plus with Eternia's power outage, it seemed almost wasteful to bother her with the small stuff. At some point, he'd have to learn when to use his lifeline correctly. For now, the skill was simply kind of there.

Skill Increased: Curse of Sacrifice
Rank: Apprentice one
I don't care about anybody else. When I think about you, I hurt myself. Oh, I don't want anybody else, oh no, oh no, oh no. I know you were singing along, but seriously, hurting yourself to cast spells has to be a real downer sometimes. On the plus side, you've made it to the apprentice ranks and picked up a new perk. Curse of Sacrifice now applies Time Bomb to the target.

When the target receives three stacks of Time Bomb, they get hit with a DOT that applies the damage of the last cast of Curse of Sacrifice over three seconds.

If I hand-picked an upgrade, it couldn't have been better.

Extra damage was nice, but the extra healing was a big deal. Tim's class was unique because he had to damage a target to activate his best healing spells. So any extra damage turned into healing, and an additional heal over time was just what the doctor ordered when it came to keeping Cassie alive.

Skill Increased: Quick Feet
Rank: Journeyman one
Run, run, Rudolph, but seriously you don't need a red nose to run fast. All you have to do is be scared or want that last popsicle from the icebox before anyone else can get their grubby little hands on it. You haven't used this skill for self-gratification, but the thrill of scooping the last dessert is always a bonus.

You've reached the journeyman ranks with this skill. Now you'll escape twenty percent faster and take ten percent reduced damage while Quick Feet is active.

Whoa, now he was going to be forty-five percent faster than

usual. That was so cool even though the skill didn't last that long. Sprinting to get out of danger was awesome, but he wondered if he could use it for other things. Tim was pretty sure getting to his first cup of coffee forty-five percent faster was a proper use of the skill, same when he wanted dibs on a seat.

The applications for other shenanigans were nearly endless.

Skill Increased: Dodge
Rank: Journeyman nine
No one likes to get hit by things, and you least of all. What initially seemed like a fluke has turned into quite the skill for you. You can jump, duck, and spin away from danger with the best of them. If your dexterity and strength were higher, you'd receive even more benefits from this.

When Dodge is active, you'll also have a ten percent chance to parry incoming physical attacks.

This skill was starting to stack the benefits. The persistent one percent dodge chance was excellent, but when he activated the skill, it now had a ten percent parry chance and a twenty percent chance of increased dodging all attacks. If he combined this skill with Quick Feet, there wasn't a boss that could touch him.

Tim chose to ignore the knock on his strength and dexterity. His other stats were way more critical, and being able to dodge at a high level was a bonus for him rather than a way of life. It sure helped when he made a mistake, or the boss got tricky, but mostly he healed his way out of trouble.

Skill Increased: Behold My Power
Rank: Master One
Congratulations on having another spell make the master ranks. Behold My Power is your strongest spell, and you use it well. While this spell does hurt your entire party, the damage it deals to the target is unparalleled. After a sacrifice as generous as a percentage of their life, our party

deserves a little bonus. When Behold My Power is activated, it applies Powershock with an added twist.

Powershock already increases the damage the spell's target takes by five percent for ten seconds. Now the target will also have all resistances lowered by five percent during that time.

Increased damage and lowered resistances were magic to Tim's ears. When the difference between winning and losing a fight could be as small as one or two percent health, every edge they could eke out mattered. He loved this spell. The only downside was he couldn't cast it all the time. It would be like having the god mode cheat from his childhood enabled.

"No power in the 'verse can stop me." Tim did his best River Tam impression and kicked his shower into overdrive.

If I take any longer, ShadowLily will send a search party.

Skill Increased: Divine Light

Rank: Master one

Whoa, when things are going good, they're really going good. Your fourth spell made the master ranks. Not only that, but it's a big-time single-target DPS spell. While Divine Light isn't exactly mana-friendly, it packs one hell of a punch. That punch now applies Light Burn.

When Light Burn is applied, the damage over time effect has a one hundred percent chance to spread to two additional targets.

Tim couldn't stop smiling as he turned off the water and stepped out of the shower. As he dried off, he thought about what the new perk to Divine Light would do. It was remarkable that the damage over time effect had a cool name like Light Burn instead of merely being a DOT. It all started by giving the damage over time effect of Divine Light a one hundred percent chance to apply instead of only twenty-five percent. That was a massive boost if there were additional enemies.

Being skilled had its privileges.

In the most recent fights, Tim used his newest skill Curse of Sacrifice more often because of the bonuses his stances gave to curses. Now Divine Light's spell cost seemed dramatically less as it spread damage to additional targets. Tim would have to pay attention to fights with at least three targets. If there were opponents, he'd work Divine Light into his damage rotation with more regularity.

Skill Increased: Who Needs a Shield
Rank: Master one
Did you earn three master-rank spells at once? With six spells in the master ranks, it won't be long until you become a grandmaster. Keep up the hard work, or in this case, keep someone else from having to do as much.

Who Needs a Shield reduces the target's damage taken by a flat ten percent for ten seconds. When the spell expires, it places a buff on the entire party called Hero's Defense.

Hero's Defense increases the entire party's dodge chance by ten percent for ten seconds. At the master ranks, it also applies a five percent increase to all magical resistances for the same timeframe.

"Holy shit!" Tim tossed his towel aside and equipped his gear.

When spells reached the master ranks, the increases were incredible. It was hard not to think about what would happen when he reached the grandmaster ranks with Healing Orb. The spell was already one of his favorites, but with an additional perk, it might make it harder for him to cast all of the other spells he needed to level.

Cassie was going to love the upgrade to Who Needs a Shield. It would also be great for those situations where they all had to run through a gauntlet of beams, orbs, and stuff on the ground that was trying to kill them. Increased resistance and the ability to dodge were keys to surviving those phases. This would be a huge advantage if he could time it right during the fights.

Facing the Sisters of Eternal Bliss would be a lot easier with all the upgrades. Not to mention Tim had a few skills that were about to reach their next milestone. Next time he updated his skills, he would have upgrades to Disturbance and Rectify. Those skills were about to hit the journeyman ranks, while Flame Burst and Healing Storm were all sitting on the edge of the master ranks. Not to mention his new class spells were quickly catching up with the rest.

Hopefully, everyone else is having the same luck I am with their updates.

Tim did a final once-over in the mirror and headed toward the door. Once he was back downstairs, it was only a matter of if the potion was ready or not. If it was, they were off on their next adventure. If it wasn't, he might sneak in some French fries and look over the list of new things he could craft. If he could make something to fill a void in the market, there was profit to gain. He loved making a profit.

If only it were as easy as rubbing my fingers together.

CHAPTER SIX

Lorelei came out of the kitchen pushing a wheelbarrow full of potions.

"Go help her." Lady Briarthorn nudged Gaston.

Gaston gave up looking broody and went to help Liz out. Since Lucy returned to the inn, he hadn't let the woman more than three feet away from him. It was as if he knew this might be the final time he got to see her.

"Where do you want it?" Gaston smiled as he picked up the handles.

Lorelei pointed, and the two of them moved as Tim tried to figure out what they might face upon their return to the sisters.

Tim laughed as the wheelbarrow full of potions went past. "That's a bit more potion than I expected."

"Tell me about it," Lorelei winked at him with a look that said at least she wasn't carrying it. "Ernie said it was cheap to make and that having more is always better than not enough."

"Did he say if it would work?" JaKobi plucked one of the blue vials from an open bag and held it up to the light.

Lorelei laughed. "I asked him the same thing, and the

grumpy old bastard said, 'I made it right, and it didn't blow up.' Then he shrugged."

"Since my man is so interested in the potion's inner workings, he's volunteered to test it out himself." Cassie thumped JaKobi on the back with a mischievous smile plastered all over her face.

The ember wizard gulped. "I will?"

"You will." Cassie kissed him. "I might forgive you for spending the last few days reading instead of with me."

"Well, I did make awesome progress on my—"

Wumph!

JaKobi rubbed his stomach. "I mean, of course, I'd like to volunteer."

"Thatta boy." Gaston set the wheelbarrow down in the center of the room. "It always pays to listen to your woman."

"Please, I do what I want." Tim said it with utter confidence but looked at ShadowLily and mumbled, "Within reason."

The mist slayer sauntered forward. "And I reserve the right to cut off anything that comes in contact with another woman."

Tim grinned. "See, we have an understanding."

Cassie laughed. "Let's divvy this stuff up and get to work."

JaKobi grabbed a handful of vials and held up something that looked like a grenade. "What. Is. This?"

Lorelei plucked the object from his hand. "*That* is a group dispersal unit."

The spirit archer bounced the grenade off her bicep and caught it. "You push the button on the top, toss it at a group of infected, and whammo, they get sprayed with the cure."

"I'll take a few of those." Tim ran up to the barrel and loaded his pockets. "What? Cleanse doesn't work on their magic, and I'm in charge of keeping everyone free of enchantments."

ShadowLily took a few blue vials and tucked them in her vest. "He *does* make a good point."

Lady Briarthorn rose from her seat by the fire and moved

to join them. "Let's get the leftovers to Grant so he can load them in the carriage."

Gaston picked up the handles to the wheelbarrow. "I'll meet you outside."

Lucy waited for Gaston to leave and turned her attention toward the group. "Thank you for doing this."

Flinging his arms wide, JaKobi motioned for everyone to bring it in close. "Group hug."

Lady Briarthorn looked aghast as the group of adventurers descended on her with their arms open. By the sheer amount of terror on Lucy's face, Tim would've thought they were trying to murder her instead of giving her comfort. The hug was brief, but he hoped Lucy knew they loved and would do anything to see the two of their friends happy.

"Did you see the look on her face!" Cassie roared with laughter.

ShadowLily bent over, howling with deep-throated chuckles of her own. "It was like she thought we were a bunch of hungry piranhas."

"Who knew anyone could be so afraid of hugs?" JaKobi leaned back in his seat and flipped to the next page in his book.

Tim's eyes turned serious. "I bet half the people she meets have a dagger in one hand and a present in the other. Being a noble is dangerous business."

"World is full of people who would rather take what's yours than work for their own." Lorelei peeked out the window. "So what's with this place anyway? Why is it so creepy?"

Looking around the carriage, Tim asked, "Anyone seen *Percy Jackson*, or maybe read a little Homer? Think lotus-eaters, but they have monsters too."

"So, what? We're going to be facing our greatest temptations and nightmares?" ShadowLily looked slightly thrilled and also like she wanted to be sick.

The truth of the matter was Tim had no idea what to expect. His time with the Sisters of Eternal Bliss was relatively pleasant until they tried to have him murdered by the thing in the lake. There was no way to know what their endgame was without confronting them. If forced to put a finger on it, he would say having the people trapped on their land was what powered their magic.

No people, no power.

At least they did it in a way that felt relatively harmless, outside the whole kidnapping thing. It wasn't that hard to sell a place with free food, drinks, and drugs to people. Especially if they didn't have to work. It certainly looked as if most people were lounging about on his last visit, but a few others had been planting and tending to the fields of crops. There was even a large bunkhouse so people didn't have to sleep outside.

If they remained stoned to the gills on stay-and-play magic, did they have the free will to leave?

Even if a person wanted to go to the Sisters of Eternal Bliss and partake in their wares, the fact they couldn't decide to leave was more than troubling. Someone might be cool staying for a day a week, even a year, but they needed to have the option to leave. Based on what Tim had seen, that wasn't the case.

"I don't know what we're going to find. All I can tell you is not to eat, drink, or smoke anything." Tim looked at each of them in turn. "Think of it as the fairy realm—you eat something, and you're never coming back."

JaKobi smiled. "If all we have to do is not eat or drink anything, why do I have to go first?"

"You've been voluntold." Cassie grinned. "Someone has to be the guinea pig for the potion."

"Can't we grab someone inside who's already affected and

give them a little sip? If it snaps them out of it, we're golden, and I don't have to end up with a tail."

"You're not going to get a tail." Cassie snickered.

Leaning close, ShadowLily whispered, "Probably."

Snapping the rope in her hands, Lorelei moved toward the wizard. "Man up, big guy."

The carriage stopped, and JaKobi turned his eyes on Tim. "Help me out here, man."

"What? If it's not you, I'm the one who's going to end up with a rope tied around his waist. I don't think so." Tim held up his hands to fend him off.

"Hey, I don't have a rope around my...." JaKobi looked at Lorelei. "Jesus, how in the fuck did you get that around my waist without me noticing?"

Lorelei patted the wizard on the shoulder, trying not to laugh. "I slipped it around your waist while you were in full panic mode."

Grant popped his head inside the door. "We're here."

Tim hopped out first. "Lorelei, tie one end of the rope around the wagon wheel. JaKobi, get ready to smoke something."

"I thought I could eat the food." JaKobi sounded a little worried about taking drugs even if they were magical.

Tim felt for the guy, and he didn't want him to be uncomfortable. "How about this? You try the food, and I'll smoke the flower."

JaKobi nodded.

"I hope it tastes awesome." Tim knew that sounded weird because JaKobi didn't know what the flower did, but he didn't want to ruin the experience for him.

Turning toward the group, Tim addressed them quickly. "JaKobi's going to go first with eating, and I'm going to try the special flower."

ShadowLily peered through the arch leading to the sisters'

land. A group of people stood around a table full of food. "I wonder if it's stronger in the food and drink like with edibles?"

"Edibles? Girl, I didn't know you did that stuff." Cassie looked mildly interested and slightly offended.

Tim couldn't tell if the tank was pissed because her best friend hadn't invited her to have a brownie or that she didn't tell her she was into them sometimes.

"During finals when I couldn't sleep, a cookie or a gummy was the only thing that eased my nerves enough to crash." ShadowLily shrugged. "Sure beats waking up with a hangover."

Tim laughed as he thought about his college roommate Xander. "Trust me. You can do both."

Lorelei looked intrigued. "Maybe we should all try it once to see how the magic and the cure affect us before an actual fight."

"I'm down with that." ShadowLily laughed as Tim quirked an eyebrow in her direction. "What? I wanna know if the potion is going to affect me in other ways before dying is on the line."

Tim drew a slow breath. They were overthinking it. "Ok, so JaKobi's going first on food and drink duty. Then we'll each go one at a time and try the flower and the antidote."

"I've never been so nervous to eat in my life." JaKobi checked the rope around his waist and walked toward the archway.

Tim gave the rope around his friend's waist a little tug. "You got this, man."

"Damn right I do." JaKobi walked through the archway with purposeful strides.

After moving under the arch to the farm, the ember wizard turned and waved at the group to let them know he was okay. It reminded Tim of the pictures at the beginning of scary movies when it showed the happy couple or the missing camper waving at their families before never being seen again.

Tim watched as his friend turned and strode toward the table. The ember wizard looked over the offerings, held up a glass of sparkling liquid to his nose, and sniffed before taking a small sip. Then he downed the entire thing and another before looking at the food. By the time Cassie hauled on the rope to pull him back, he'd eaten three brownies and was reaching for a fourth.

"That antidote better be strong." Tim thought about the time he ate a not so properly dosed brownie and slept for an entire day.

JaKobi was fighting against the pull of the rope, trying to get back to the table. Growling in frustration, he turned and burned a hole in the rope. Cassie and ShadowLily fell to the ground in a heap, and JaKobi grabbed another glass from the table.

"Stay with me, and don't eat anything." Tim ran, and Lorelei followed him.

Lorelei circled behind JaKobi as Tim called to him to grab his attention. "Hey buddy, what are you doing?"

"Dude, you gotta try the brownies. They taste like heaven. Each bite is a vanilla apple pie orgasm in my mouth." JaKobi shoved another full brownie into his mouth.

Lorelei laughed from behind the ember wizard as she pulled him into a hold he couldn't break free of. "That's why I never date men, all the mouth explosions."

Struggling against the hold she had him in, JaKobi couldn't help but giggle. That was when Tim rushed forward and dumped the potion into his mouth. Lorelei let go, and JaKobi dropped to his knees. With a heave, he threw up all of his brownies.

"Not worth it." The ember wizard moaned as Tim healed him. "Oh, it really wasn't worth it."

Cassie bent to help him up. "Not sure if I want to try the potion now."

Lorelei had already picked up one end of a hookah and was puffing contentedly away. "Ummm, cafe mocha with java chip ice cream. It's like I'm smoking a memory."

Tim shook a vial in her face. "Have you tried the liquid version yet? It's far out."

"No way." Lorelei snatched the vial and drank the contents in one swallow.

Swaying for a moment, Lorelei fell on her butt. "Reality is so...depressing."

"At least you didn't throw up." JaKobi rubbed his mouth on his sleeve and sent his robe through the inventory trick to clean it.

Tim looked from the hookah to the food and mused, "The food and drink must be more concentrated."

"To keep from barfing, I'm going with the hookah." ShadowLily picked up the mouthpiece and took a gentle puff. "Lemon blueberry cake with cream cheese frosting."

The spell took hold. "Please," she whined. "Tell me I don't have to stop."

"Of course you don't, babe. You only need to stay hydrated." Tim held up a vial of the antidote.

ShadowLily grabbed the vial. "Thanks for looking out for me." Then she drank it.

A moment later, she was sitting right next to Lorelei. "Now, I get it."

"Right?" The spirit archer replied casually, still sounding a little down.

"If this is going to suck, I'm getting it out of the way." Cassie grabbed her mouthpiece and took a hit.

Doing the Snoopy happy dance, Cassie continued to puff. "Oh my God, it's like I'm eating a cheeseburger and having a strawberry shake at the same time."

JaKobi moved forward. "You know, the only thing you're

missing is a little of this." He popped the cork off and pretended to sip.

Snatching the vial from his hands, Cassie drank the contents in one quick gulp and fell to her knees. "Oh, dear."

Tim moved forward and picked up the mouthpiece. He loaded a little bit of new flower into the burner and puffed. It felt like he was riding on a springtime cloud, and everything would be right in the world.

He took another pull from the hookah, letting the smoke out with a contented sigh. "Peanut butter and jelly with bacon."

"I'm not sure that counts as a win." JaKobi waggled another vial of antidote from side to side. "How about you wash that down with a little blueberry lemonade?"

Tim grabbed the container and scoffed at his friend. "Just because you've never tasted the amazing combination of salty bacon mixed with creamy peanut butter and strawberry jelly doesn't mean it isn't awesome."

With a quick flip of his wrist, he downed the contents. "Doesn't taste like blueberries."

He did feel a little down, but it wasn't that bad. This wasn't depression exactly. It was more of that feeling when a person was excited to get something, and when it came, it wasn't the correct version, and they had to wait for a replacement. It was depression adjacent. The real question was would another dose of the antidote make it better, or was this as good as it got?

Tim opened another vial as they walked back toward the carriage. He drank this one a little slower. The taste was terrible but not as bad as the medicine he used to take as a kid. His mood didn't change, and no adverse status effects showed when he checked, so he must simply be missing his favorite sandwich more than he thought. When they got back to Joe's, he would place a special order.

The adventurers stood around the carriage while Cassie untied the rope from the wheel. "This is it, guys. We're heading in for real this time. No matter what you feel, do not eat, drink, or smoke anything."

"If I ever see another brownie it'll be too soon." JaKobi looked queasy at the idea of food.

ShadowLily put her hands on her hips. "I think I'll be able to restrain myself."

"Then let's go find the sisters and see what they have to say for themselves." Tim looked at Lorelei and held out his hand. "Blue Daggers on three."

The spirit archer squealed with delight. "I love these."

"Can't disappoint her." JaKobi placed his hand on top of Tim's.

When everyone was in a circle, hands stacked on top of each other, Tim started the countdown. "One, two, three."

"Blue Daggers for life!" they roared in unison.

CHAPTER SEVEN

"Hey, do you think these grenades work on other people than us?" JaKobi asked as they passed a group of ten people sitting around a table eating tacos with bowls of ice cream on standby.

Cassie pulled one of the creations off her belt and tossed it at the group. "Only one way to find out."

The grenade flew through the air, landing about ten feet short of the people. It took one significant bounce and two smaller ones before rolling to a stop at one of the men's feet. He bent and picked up the grenade. Tim got ready to heal him if there was an explosion.

The man held the grenade up in front of his face and smiled. "Far out." He turned to his friends. "Look what I found."

Blue mist shot from the grenade and covered the area around the man who picked it up in a ten-foot circle of antidote mist. Slowly the group emerged from the cloud of gas, looking dazed. More than a few of them got sick. Tim healed them all and cast Cleanse in case they were suffering from any other ailments.

"Follow the path back to the exit." Tim pointed back the way they'd come. "Don't eat, drink, or smoke anything."

"Okay, Dad." One of the men snickered.

A woman hit him in the gut hard enough he doubled over. "It was your bright idea that got us stuck here in the first place."

The group walked down the path, and another of the women grumbled.

"I must have been an idiot to let you tie that rope around my waist."

Tim looked at JaKobi. "Sorry, broski."

"Bah, it was fun. I'll never forget the taste of those brownies." JaKobi sighed contentedly.

Cassie snorted. "Just remember what happens afterward."

"Might be worth it.' JaKobi looked like he was considering eating another one when he spun. "Did you get a quest update?"

Quest Update: Tit for Tat

You've freed ten people from the clutches of the sisters' magic. Free a hundred more people from the Sisters of Eternal Bliss for an additional reward.

Reward: ten gold coins and a bar of blessed steel.

"Heck yeah, I did." Tim was already thinking about what he might be able to craft with the reward.

Cassie thumped her staff on the hard dirt trail to get all of their attention. "If we have a quest and now a side quest, that means shit is about to get real. Let's free as many as we can before things get too crazy."

"Someone's not going to be happy when their guests leave." Lorelei shrugged and pointed down the trail. "Kind of like that guy. He looks downright pissed."

The man walking down the trail certainly looked peeved about something. Tim was almost more interested in his outfit than his surly disposition. Maybe it was the frayed overalls or the fact he only had them buttoned on one side that made him think country boy, but nothing sealed it like the fact he wasn't wearing shoes.

A small cringe twisted at the corners of Tim's lips as the man stepped on a rock in the path. The man didn't miss a beat as he kept going. The soles of his feet must have been as tough as Tim's boots. His feet preferred carpet or a rug. Anything else, and he had socks on. The man on the trail waved, pulling Tim's mind away from starting to list his favorite types of carpet.

"Turn around. You're not welcome here!" the man shouted as he ran down the trail.

Cassie moved to the front of the group. "Battle positions."

As the man closed the distance, Tim had time to scan him. Brian Dallas, retention specialist.

"Boss fight!" Tim screamed at the top of his lungs.

There was always a chance he could be wrong, but he tended to be spot on about these sorts of things. Now that the team knew what was potentially coming their way, they could prepare their attacks accordingly. They used a different strategy for a boss than when they were nuking a set of trash mobs.

Boss fights were their bread and butter.

As the retention specialist ran toward them, he doubled in size, and his lackluster wardrobe turned into a suit of shining armor complete with a sword and shield.

"Am I the only one seeing this?" Cassie questioned as she set her feet to meet the boss' charge.

ShadowLily winked out of existence. "If you mean did I see him go from all cute and farmery to a solid chunk of steel, I sure did."

Cassie's staff *clanged* against the retention specialist's sword. The two of them tested each other out with a few more blows before the group jumped in to help. Tim started by casting Curse of Giving and Behold My Power. It felt reckless to start with his most powerful spell, but he was tired of saving it for the end of fights.

Lorelei disappeared and popped into existence fifteen feet away with a volley of attacks into the retention specialist's side.

A phoenix made of pure flames flew over Tim's head as JaKobi joined the fray. Then it was time for him to start paying real attention to everyone's health. He sent out a trio of Healing Orb and cast Curse of Sacrifice on the boss as he tried to get the lay of the land. Right now it was only them and the boss, but they were in a wide-open field, so it might not stay that way for long.

What good was a specialist if he didn't have a support group to handle the day-to-day?

The group was taking slow, intermittent damage, more than what Behold My Power would do on its own. It stressed his single-target healing, so instead of trying to heal his way out of it, he looked for the problem's cause. None of their group had a negative status effect that he could see, so it must be something the boss was casting. Tim scanned the retention specialist and saw a single unremovable debuff.

Deceitful Retribution: So the cherished will know the strength of our love. When a villain comes calling, they will be encased in a shell of righteous anger. Any damage done unto them will be partially reflected back on the perpetrator.

That's a lot of words for a simple thorns skill.

His internal timer for Behold My Power went off, and there were only a few seconds left before the effect would trigger. He cast Hex of the Shattered Beast on Cassie and Who Needs a Shield on himself as he waited for the damage spike to hit him.

The boss' health dropped a full five percent, but Tim's dropped sixty, and that was with the protection of Who Needs a Shield. If he hadn't activated the skill, he might've died. With all his defensive spells on cooldown, he would have to think about what skills to use going forward so he didn't damage his health beyond repair.

So much for being bold.

Tim cast Healing Storm to top everyone off before replenishing his trio of Healing Orb. Despite the early mistakes, his mana pool looked fat and healthy, and everyone's health was above ninety percent except for his and the boss'. Despite the retention specialist's best efforts, he wasn't making any progress against their group.

ShadowLily waited for the boss to swing and rolled closer to him before he could lift his arm again. Her daggers scraped against the thick metal armor until one of them slipped inside a joint. As the retention specialist pulled his arm back, ShadowLily rolled with it and renewed her attacks from behind the boss, looking for another opening.

If the asshole wasn't trying to kill us, I might feel bad for him.

If there was one thing he'd been begging for since they entered the game, it was a simple tank and spank fight. Maybe he'd finally gotten his wish. The boss was approaching seventy-five percent health, and outside of Tim's early mistakes, the rest of the group hadn't struggled at all. The real kicker would be whatever the boss' special ability was. If it was big, the fight might not be as simple as it appeared now.

"Enough!" The retention specialist broke free from Cassie's and ShadowLily's attacks and took a step back. "Maybe it was wrong of me to try to ban you from the property. With skills like those your group would be an incredible asset for the community."

Cassie spat on the ground. "What, now you're trying to hire us?"

"Refreshments." The retention specialist clapped his hands, and a group of ten people appeared bearing trays of food, drinks, or smokable flowers for them to sample.

One of the brand ambassadors spoke, and all of them repeated her words in unison. "You should be one of us."

They repeated "one of us" every few steps they took toward the group.

JaKobi held out his arms like he was in *Invasion of the Body Snatchers* or *Hot Fuzz*. "One of us."

"Fuck off and get the antidotes out for me." Lorelei tapped a hand against his chest. "Give me one of those grenades."

JaKobi pulled a grenade from his inventory and handed it to her. "Make a good throw."

"I never do anything short of perfection." Lorelei tossed the grenade, and it arced high into the air.

When the weapon was above the group's center, it detonated, covering the area in blue mist. Tim's counter went from ten to twenty people saved as the group of former brand ambassadors staggered out of the mist heading toward the exit.

"You know when you do those things, you put us all at risk. You put me at risk," the retention specialist growled. "I'm responsible for growing the herd and seeing to its happiness."

Swinging his sword around in a giant arc, the retention specialist charged forward. "I hate when people fuck with my shit."

Cassie blocked his first swing with casual grace. "Get used to disappointment."

A blast of pure light struck the boss in the chest. Then Cassie was on him. It was like watching a kid play street hockey with a tin can for the puck. Her staff rose and fell, and with each metal *clank*, the retention specialist seemed more vulnerable than ever before. His health was coming off in good solid chunks, and despite the man's giant shield, they almost had him down to fifty percent.

There was tank and spank, and there was set up for a trap. Tim wasn't sure exactly which group they would fall into yet.

He kept up with his heals and continued moving his eyes around the landscape, looking for any surprises.

The first time they attempted a fight it was always hard to guess what would happen next. It was a sign of good development, but it also made each skirmish unique enough to be difficult. Until Tim knew the lay of the land, he was a big fan of playing it safe. If this fight ended up being super easy, maybe they would pop back into the instance and do it again. They didn't have the luxury of doing loot runs right now since the game kept them moving at a quick pace, but once they reached the level cap, this guy would become their bitch for some weekly freebies.

The retention specialist backed off again as his health hit fifty percent.

His shield and sword disappeared, and he looked down at his empty hands with a confused expression. "I don't know why you're fighting against us so hard. All we want to do is give you a place where you can be free to be yourself with no judgment."

"Judgment and sarcasm are what I eat for breakfast." ShadowLily stared the boss down.

Cassie ruined the effect when she snickered. "Is that what you're calling them now?"

Tim slapped his forehead. "My balls are not called Judgment and Sarcasm."

"Try to be more receptive to my proposal." The retention specialist ignored their byplay completely. "Let me offer you additional refreshments."

Twenty people appeared on the hill and descended toward them. Some of them were flashing red.

"Oh, it seems some of our brand ambassadors aren't too happy with you." The retention specialist laughed. "Better watch out. They get pretty explosive."

Lorelei snickered. "They should try reading the gaming forums."

The group laughed as the spirit archer held out her hand. "Give me a couple of those grenades."

Tim watched as the first grenade sailed into the crowd of people and shuddered. Sure, they were only trying to blast them with an antidote, but he couldn't shake off all those war movies and shows he'd seen. *Seriously, was there anything more brutal than The Pacific?* He didn't want to end up tossing rocks into a skull. He liked his fun times a little lighter than pitch black.

At least this battle was going better than Jack Napier's day.

The second grenade went off, and Tim's status updated to thirty-five of a hundred freed. He did some quick math as people emerged from the blue cloud and realized they hadn't cured them all. Maybe they couldn't fix the red ones. If they weren't curable, they were a big problem.

"This fight might not be so easy after all," Tim whispered as he watched the cloud. In a much louder voice, he addressed the group. "Get ready for trouble."

The group moved into a more traditional battle formation with Cassie at the front. All of them were peering into the hazy cloud of antidote, waiting to see when the first of the five would emerge. Tim had no idea what was going to happen. Were the brand ambassadors infected? Would they blow up? Too many scenarios were spinning through his mind. He was starting to lose his cool.

The first red-tinted brand ambassador came out of the blue mist charging straight at Cassie. She threw the giant platter of French fries at the tank, and the shadow dancer batted it out of the way. Fries flew everywhere like a kid throwing a food tantrum.

Two wiry arms wrapped around Cassie's waist, and before she could dislodge the brand ambassador, the woman screamed, "Don't forget to leave a five-star review!" and exploded.

Red mist swallowed the tank, and when she turned, her eyes were glowing red. "You should consider staying. This place is fucking awesome."

ShadowLily appeared behind Cassie and grabbed her head, forcing it back enough to dump a vial of antidote into her mouth. "Don't let them buy you with free swag."

It was hard not to laugh. Even in *The Etheric Coast,* reviews mattered.

Cassie fell to her knees gagging, and ShadowLily turned, scanning the mist for the next brand ambassador. Looking from the blue haze back to Cassie, Tim gave up watching for the next attack and started healing. Healing Orb took care of the worst of the damage, and he'd be able to cast it again soon. He let the DOT effect tick as he checked Cassie for status effects.

Weakness to Marketing: after succumbing to the brand ambassadors' efforts to retain you as a client, all stats are reduced by ten percent for one minute.

Cleanse didn't take the debuff away, and it was too big a hit for them to risk the spell affecting any of the others. This was a fight, and sometimes in big fights, sacrifices had to be made. He didn't like it but stopping the Sisters of Eternal Bliss and staying alive were his top priorities, not saving every person the vile bitches ensnared.

Even if he wanted to.

"Everyone back up. We'll take them out from range." Tim cast his next Healing Orb as he shuffled backward a few paces.

Cassie fell back as the next brand ambassador ran out of the mist. "I have a twenty percent discount."

JaKobi incinerated him and pointed to the right.

"I'll get you upgraded for free." Her pitch faded to gurgles as an arrow appeared in her throat.

The blue mist parted. "Don't forget to use my affiliate code for a discount."

Tim cast Flame Burst as a throwing knife slammed into the woman's chest. 'Good to see we're on the same page."

"Nothing I hate worse than a pushy salesman." ShadowLily was already watching the mist for the last threat.

With a shriek of rage, the last brand ambassador ran from the dispersing cloud of antidote. "Don't you want to be as popular as me?"

"Fuck no, I can buy my own damn brownies." Tim cast Curse of Sacrifice and tried not to giggle maniacally as five different attacks hit at once, blowing the ambassador apart.

Back in the real world, he would've loved to blast every telemarketer back into the Stone Age. Here he was getting the chance.

Video games were so fucking cool!

With his minions gone, the retention specialist charged back into battle, a new smaller sword held high above his head. A blue glow wreathed the entire blade marking it as magical. The same blue light shone at the edges of his shield. The shield had also shrunk from a large tower shield to a small round buckler. Times were tough for Mr. Dallas. The full plate mail armor he proudly sported was now a pair of rusty gauntlets and pauldrons. The rest of the magical armor had disappeared, and he was back in the comfy-looking overalls with no shoes.

Spitting out the piece of grass he was sucking on, the boss screamed, "You should be nicer to our associates. They only have your best interests at heart."

"This is like one of those timeshares you can't get out of." Cassie deflected a series of rapid strikes. "Listen, asshole. We're not interested."

Tim was behind on his healing, and the group showed signs of strain. He'd been so involved in doing damage he forgot that everyone was taking damage from the boss' special ability. A quick trio of Healing Orb got things back on track, and a burst of Healing Storm set everything right. His mana was a little worse for wear but dealing with the brand ambassadors gave him time to recharge.

The boss wasn't doing so well now that his armor was mostly gone. He'd been able to hold Cassie and ShadowLily at bay before, but now when one of their attacks slipped past, there wasn't any armor to stop it. JaKobi and Lorelei were hammering the bastard with everything they had. With Tim's magical attacks contributing damage, the boss' health was dropping faster than expected. An arrow stuck out of the retention specialist's leg, and scorch marks covered his overalls.

"I've tried the nice approach, but now I'm going to make you an offer you can't refuse," Brian Dallas screeched as he leapt away from the group.

Thirty people appeared behind him, slowly making their way down the hill. Twenty of them were average Joes, but red edges tinged five of them, and blue tinted another five. The blue ones were the only unknown they had to deal with so Tim didn't have time to overthink it. He needed to make a quick decision.

"Lorelei and JaKobi, drop all the red ones." Tim turned to Cassie and ShadowLily. "You two grab grenades and come with me."

The NPCs outlined in red blew up as the group of brand ambassadors continued their trek down the hill. They covered the area with more red mist. Two blue ones ran through the spray and were now purple-tinged.

Shit, now we have two problems to deal with.

"Grenades." Tim threw two of his, and Cassie and Lorelei filled in the gaps with theirs.

The counter on his quest went up to forty-five, and Tim

knew all that was left were the new additions and the three remaining blue-tinged ambassadors.

The mist from their grenades dissipated quickly, revealing a new monstrosity they had to deal with. While shrouded in the antidote, the three blue brand ambassadors merged into one gigantic person. A large platform was attached to the new monster's back with two giant slings resting on his shoulders. The two purple-outlined ambassadors rode atop it with huge trays of cupcakes and brownies. They loaded the treats into their slings and flung them at the group as the Blue Daggers scattered.

"Everyone loves a free sample," one of the women cried with glee.

The second woman cackled. "You can't represent our product correctly until you use it yourself."

The monstrosity of a man growled, "One of us!"

"You know what I love about this?" Cassie smugly grinned as she looked back at her friends. "The bigger they are..."

"Go get him, baby!" JaKobi screamed as he watched his girlfriend charge past the cupcakes to bring the fight in close.

Lorelei fired an arrow that split into four parts and kept the women from using their slings as ShadowLily scrambled up the monstrosity's back to get to them. The two ambassadors didn't stand a chance.

The big bastard was giving Cassie everything she could handle, but their tank wasn't fighting alone. ShadowLily stopped trying to kill the women on the platform and instead shoved them off the side where it would be easier for Lorelei and JaKobi to pick them off. With the two women out of the way, the monstrosity didn't stand a chance. The creature's magic faded with a loud *pop*, dumping the three blue brand ambassadors to the ground.

The three men rushed to their feet and wrapped their arms around Cassie as if they wanted to give her a giant hug.

The tank's eyes pulsed with blue light. "Guys, this stuff is the best!"

The men smiled as they spread out and spoke in one voice. "Can we get your friends some additional refreshments?"

They lifted their hands like Iron Man, but instead of a beam of light, bright blue liquid sprayed from their hands. ShadowLily danced back as the retention specialist charged in from a different direction. Without a tank to help them, the group was in a bad place.

Tim switched his Way of the Boulder stance from Cassie to ShadowLily and cast his heals. Curse of Giving went on all the remaining blue men and the boss. With four periodic heals on her, ShadowLily held her own against the continued assault.

The boss' armor was completely gone now, and he'd shrunk back to normal human size. His colossal sword had turned back into a walking stick. The three men ran toward JaKobi now, trying to engulf him in their spell as they had with Cassie. The first one grabbed his legs and tried to pull him back to the other men.

The only way to stop the effect was to kill the boss. With no armor, ShadowLily's daggers were ripping huge pieces of flesh from the retention specialist. It didn't take long for the boss' health to reach zero. She'd destroyed him almost on her own.

The blue glow around the men holding JaKobi to the ground faded and winked out.

"Us girls gotta stick together." Lorelei flung a grenade at Cassie.

Cassie came out of the cloud coughing. "Oh, that's nasty."

A cloud engulfed the three remaining brand ambassadors. They emerged from the mist, talking and laughing among themselves as they headed toward the exit. Tim's counter went up by another three people, and he turned back to where the boss died. Instead of a body, there was a large golden chest.

Long live the Blue Dagger Society.

CHAPTER EIGHT

"Well, that was different." Tim kept his eyes focused on the chest.

JaKobi laughed. "Going online is almost worse than opening the front door these days."

Cassie moved toward the chest with a gleam in her eye. "Who would have thought the Sisters of Eternal Bliss would work so hard to keep people here?"

Everyone else raised their hands, and they all broke out in laughter.

At least they'd learned something from the fight. The sisters' magical strength had at least a partial base in the number of people under their influence. For the adventurers, it simply meant the more people they freed on the way to their next fight, the easier it would be. It might be worth taking a small detour to inoculate as many people as possible.

It would be nice if this entire dungeon were a loot crawl. It didn't often happen in games, but there was an instance now and again, or two players gravitated to it for gearing up new players. Maybe they'd found their magical loot spot, and the key was simply to vaccinate as many folks as possible from the sisters' influence.

"I know that look on your face." Cassie was watching Tim like a hawk. "Let's get the loot out of the way before you tell us what's rolling around in that big brain of yours."

Tim grinned. "When size matters, I'm packing a large."

"Yeah, boy!" JaKobi jumped and high-fived him.

Cassie laid her hand on the chest, completely ignoring the two of them as they bro'd down. "Gauntlets of the Dexterous Destroyer. Long story short, I'm a bigger badass than I was a few seconds ago."

"I can't let you have all the fun." ShadowLily moved toward the chest, flipped over the top of it, and placed her hand on the other side.

JaKobi watched the flip with a longing expression. "Show-off."

"Don't be jelly," ShadowLily admonished, wagging her finger. "If you want the goods, get over here."

Running forward, JaKobi leapt at the chest. His foot caught on the top edge, and he ended up in a heap on top of ShadowLily.

Trying to play it off like the crash was what he planned all along, the ember wizard looked into her eyes and casually asked, "So, what did you get?"

Rolling out from under him, ShadowLily popped back to her feet and pulled him up with a smile on her face. "I got a new pair of gloves." She tapped him on the chest, showing off the gloves to everyone. "Maybe save the acrobatics for me next time."

JaKobi equipped his new boots. "I don't know. In these boots, it feels like I could do anything."

"Just make sure to warn us before you try." Lorelei grinned at the ember wizard as he stuck his tongue out.

The spirit archer's face brightened as she rested her hand

on the chest. "Whoa, I got a ring and necklace. Together they have an additional effect that can supercharge one of my attacks by ten percent once per encounter."

Tim moved forward. "That's awesome. If we all have something like that, we should stagger it or save it for the last ten percent."

"Get your loot and enlighten us as to what you've been thinking about since the fight ended." Cassie tapped her foot impatiently.

Taking his time to walk up to the chest, Tim stopped in front of it and turned. "Maybe I should tell you now."

Cassie grabbed his hand and put it on the chest with a grin. "Tell us after."

"Someone's in a hurry," Tim quipped as he looked over the item screen.

Item Received: Band of Retention

Arlic the Mad was a great wizard with a shoddy mana pool. Unable to cast as many spells as his fellow wizards, he came up with the improbable idea of magical feedback. Instead of causing pain, he wanted to harness some of the mana from the spell he'd just cast. He drove himself mad testing out the prototypes, but in the end, he successfully created this magical band of electrum.

+3 Endurance +2 Dexterity, Special ability: mana feedback

After successfully casting a spell, five percent of the spell's cost will return to you.

Tim placed the bangle on his wrist as the chest disappeared. "You're not going to believe this."

"You didn't get another set-piece, did you?" JaKobi sounded envious of his luck.

Laughing at the absurdity of it, Tim told his buddy what it was. "Reduced mana cost for spells."

"Holy shit." JaKobi looked at where the chest had been. "Where's mine?"

Tim wrapped an arm around his friend's shoulders and started walking. "Coming up, my friend. It's coming up."

There was a large barn in the distance, and their path was taking them straight to it. Every couple hundred feet, there was a way station with food and flowers for consumption. Most of the stations were empty, but now and then they ran into someone they freed with a vial of antidote. Tim's counter for the quest was now sitting at sixty.

Tim kept his eyes moving all around the horizon, looking for signs of a threat, but nothing concerning jumped out.

Pointing into the distance where the big red farmhouse stood, Lorelei announced, "Hey, something's going on over there. It's a lot of people, and they don't look happy."

"That's different. I thought everyone here was happy." ShadowLily moved faster.

Cassie was right behind her, fingering the pin on an antidote grenade. "We're about to finish that side quest early."

"If Lorelei's right, we might not get credit. It sounds like these folks stopped drinking the Kool-Aid." Tim tugged on JaKobi's sleeve. "Come on, let's go."

The ember wizard started to jog. "I'm going to have to get a flying carpet or something because this running stuff is starting to get ridiculous."

Mounts! Holy shit, did this game have mounts?

They had carriages in the city and horses they could ride to destinations. There had to be something they could find that he could ride around in instances. Even games that didn't have mounts often had fun little items or potions that increased out-of-combat speed and endurance. No one liked slogging around. The fun part was the fighting.

They ran after the three women, doing their best to keep up, but they fell behind. By the time they caught up, the women were already talking to some of the gathered people and getting information. None of the milling people seemed to be stoned or want any part of the delectable treats on the table.

What in the fuck was going on?

ShadowLily broke away from the pack. "It sounds like a monster ate some people. Snapped everyone out of their daze real quick."

Tim looked around. He didn't see any signs of a monster or an attack, but everyone was agitated and not under the influence of the sisters' spell. An attack made the most sense, but why hadn't the herd been sedated again? Was it because his team killed the retention specialist?

There was no one to take control of the confused people so it was up to his group to do it. Tim opened his mouth, but Cassie let out a shrill whistle. Everyone milling around turned to face her, hoping she had some answers.

"Listen up. The exit is that way." Cassie turned and pointed back the way they'd come. "Follow the path, and don't eat, drink, or smoke anything."

When the crowd didn't move, Cassie growled, "You got me?"

Without any better options, since none of them wanted to tangle with the angry-looking tank, the people filed past them. They moved in dribs and drabs at first, but then small groups broke away like the side of an iceberg. Soon the Blue Daggers couldn't stop the flow.

Near the end of the line, Tim grabbed a man wearing a royal crest on his tunic. "Can you tell us anything more about what happened here?"

Looking back at an open field, the man pointed at a gnarled tree stump. "That stump...it came alive, and it ate someone."

"He's been smoking that funk." Lorelei laughed. "Tree stumps don't eat people."

JaKobi laughed. "People eat people, so anything is possible."

"Someone ate me this morning," ShadowLily quipped as she disappeared.

Cassie whirled to smack her but frowned when the assassin was gone. "TMI, bitch!"

Tim held out his hands in a "calm down" gesture, but he wanted to change the subject as quickly as possible. "Why don't we go check out that stump?"

The spirit archer moved toward the fence, jumped on top, and looked out over the field. "There is some blood out there, but the field itself doesn't look disturbed."

"Could be magic." JaKobi moved to join her by the fence. "Anything is possible with magic, and this place is evil enough to have tree stump monsters."

Cassie tugged her vest down and marched toward the open gate. "Only one way to find out."

"Form up on Cassie and be ready for surprises." Tim got into position. "Cast those pesky buffs.."

A wave of energy washed over him as he followed Cassie into the field. The buffs weren't much individually, but when stacked, they made a big difference to his stats. It was lucky that they had such a well-balanced party because they had boosts to almost every primary stat. The only thing they were lacking was a boost to strength.

The field looked like any recently harvested piece of land. There were ruts from the previous crop's planting, and bits of leaves and scraps littered the ground. The tilled earth around the stump was clear of plants, but even from thirty feet back, Tim could make out the splatters of blood on the ground. He wondered if the farmers hadn't removed the stump because it was too expensive or because it ate them when they tried.

Sometimes it was easier to work around a problem.

Cassie knelt and picked up a rock, and with a simple flick of her wrist, winged the stone at the stump. The large rock *clunked* off it, landing in the field a few feet away. Nothing happened for a moment. Then the ground started to shake. Dirt fell from the stump like rain as it rose from the ground.

The stump turned out to be something attached to the back of a giant beetle. The thing had to be twelve feet long, and its pincers added another five feet of razor-sharp death. Swinging the pincers around to ensure it wasn't under immediate threat, the boss faced the group.

Stumpy: Giver of Bountiful Harvests

Tim would've laughed at the giant beetle's name if the sisters weren't sacrificing people to it to improve their yields. It wasn't hard to imagine that most of the time, the people working the field were simply too stoned to notice when Stumpy decided to eat someone. That, or they thought they were having a bad trip. There was always a chance that defeating the retention specialist broke some of the sisters' hold, and this was the result.

Cassie glanced back at Tim. "You ready to do this?"

"Let's get it on," Tim replied like an old-time boxing announcer as he readied his first spell.

Not wasting time with her reply, Cassie charged into battle. Rolling under the pincers, she brought her staff up into the boss' armored belly and redirected the energy into a blow to the creature's leg. Surprisingly, ShadowLily wasn't far behind this time, jumping into the fight well before she normally would. Her daggers weren't as effective against the beetle's armored legs, but it wouldn't be long before she found a way to climb the creature's back and strike from above.

Curse of Giving and Hex of the Shattered Beast were the

first two spells that tumbled from Tim's lips. He followed it up with his standard trio of Healing Orb and sat back to observe the fight.

JaKobi was blasting Stumpy with wave after wave of fire, but the flames were ineffective against the creature's thick carapace. The stump, on the other hand, was having one hell of a time. The fire had ignited the remains, and now the wood was *crackling*. Lorelei fired an arrow into it, and a few seconds later, it exploded.

The boss crashed to the ground, and Cassie and ShadowLily hammered its defenseless body relentlessly. As Stumpy regained its feet, its back erupted, and a horde of angry wasps flew out of the wooden remains. Before the swarm could spread, JaKobi melted them in a beam of pure sunlight.

Tim drew a deep breath and let out a sigh of relief right as Stumpy started to shake. The dirt and the tree stump remains fell from the beetle's back, and two giant wings buzzed, pushing them all to the field's edge. The boss turned again and flapped its wings at them. Something flew off, but there was no way to know what it was.

Tim tried to move, but a barrier in front of them kept them in place. It didn't stop him from getting the group up to full health, but they weren't allowed to rejoin the fight yet.

Plants bloomed at the far end of the field as Stumpy faced them. There didn't appear to be a set pattern, but soon the blooming plants exploded. Then the barrier dropped, and the Blue Daggers ran forward.

"There's a safe zone by the boss," Tim called as he tried to keep up with the others.

Plants bloomed behind him as he ran. They didn't concern him. Anything happening behind him wasn't a threat unless one of them got all explode-y while he was right next to it. Then it'd be like someone pulling the pin on a grenade and shoving it down his pants.

Not fucking pretty.

It didn't take long for the blooming flower to overtake him, and Tim had to pay attention. A trio of Healing Orb went out to the group as he dodged to the left. Then an explosion to his right sent him stumbling. He bounced off a flower and hit the deck as the plant exploded. He didn't lose an arm, but he wondered how much skin was required to consider it still attached.

The only thing that got him back on his feet and running was the periodic healing provided by Hydrate. A few steps later, there was more than a bit of skin holding his arm in place. Another Healing Orb and a burst of Healing Storm, and he was almost as good as new. The rest of the group was in a similar situation except for JaKobi, who was burning a path through the explosive vegetation and not taking a single tick of damage.

"Slow and steady wins the race." JaKobi grinned as he made it into the protective circle before anyone else.

Tim was the last one in, and he didn't have time to do anything more than cast Healing Storm before Cassie was back on Stumpy. For a mini-boss, this bastard was putting up a fight. The mini-bosses in raids or dungeons were normally easy wins, but now and then, the developers liked to stick it to the players because a mini-boss being too hard didn't mean they couldn't complete the instance.

This would've been one of those cases, but Stumpy was already at thirty-five percent health. There was no way they were getting out of this fight without winning. Tim cast Curse of Sacrifice to help out with the damage and dropped Behold My Power simultaneously. Then it was his job to simply keep everyone else alive as he waited for the big blast of damage from his hardest-hitting spell.

Stumpy hit twenty percent, and Behold My Power instantly

dropped him to fifteen. The boss' legs twitched to indicate a special attack.

"Interrupt," Tim cried as he cast Disturbance.

Everyone used their interrupt simultaneously, so they had to find a way to kill the giant man-eating beetle before it could use that particular skill again. ShadowLily was on the bug's head hacking at an antenna while Cassie did her best to hammer a crack in one of Stumpy's pincers. Arrows appeared in any gaps made in the carapace, and JaKobi blasted them with fire to do more damage.

Stumpy's health plummeted to five percent, and his wings flapped again as he spun in a circle like a bucking horse.

"Give him everything you've got. We can't survive another round of exploding plants." Tim cast Divine Light on repeat, hoping it would be enough to pull them through.

His mana was totally in the shitter now, but it wasn't in as bad a shape as Stumpy's health. The boss sent his seeds out into the field, and the plants bloomed all around them. The flowers *popped* one by one, but it was too late to save the boss. The fight was over. Stumpy was dead.

CHAPTER NINE

Gaston smiled as he wiped down the bar.

Lady Briarthorn left a few hours ago to return home. She'd been gone long enough that others would've noticed any further delay. A lady was allowed to have a few moments of heartache over an arranged marriage, but anything longer than that would be considered an affront to the groom.

Not that Liam Ravenstorm was worthy of being her husband.

That rat-faced weasel was the worst kind of man. It didn't take any talent to win battles when you always did it with overwhelming force. Safety in numbers and riches protected the little shit long enough. There were plenty of contracts open on his life, but every assassin in Promethia knew better than to attack a noble. Especially one as powerful as the duke's son.

It never paid to bite the hand that feeds, and the nobles were their best clients.

With their order responsible for taking care of the nobles' dirty work, they held a lot of their secrets as well. It was a fragile balance that kept the city guard from trying to wipe them out, but it was an alliance they maintained willingly. Not that Duke Ravenstorm cared one shit for their rules. Her gold had seduced some of their order's younger members to take action. He'd done his best to end it, but it didn't matter if it was the assassin's guild who did the killing when the victim had a knife wound in their back.

Extra eyes watching the guild was never a good thing when their job was to hide in the shadows.

Ditching the rag in the bucket under the bar, Gaston waved at Liz. "I'll be back in ten. Have to go across the street for a bit."

"If you're going to see that lady of yours, you can have a few hours." The look on Liz's face made it clear she thought their relationship was the perfect love story, and she would do anything to keep it going.

Gaston smiled as he thought about Lucy's full figure. "Sadly, it's other business that calls me."

"Give 'em hell, big guy." Liz poured a beer and slid it down the bar.

It was nice to work somewhere that he felt appreciated. It wasn't always easy to find new friends when they found out he killed people for a living. Not everyone was comfortable introducing their friend the assassin at dinner parties. At the Blue Dagger Inn, he didn't have to worry about any of that. This was where he would always be accepted.

Gaston ran a crew of assassins and trained with them daily. The murderball in his basement wasn't only there to give the players something to talk about. It was a valuable training tool. An assassin never knew where the next job would take them and what skills they would need to complete the task, so they became jacks of all trades.

All of them had their specialties, too.

He stepped out in the rain, thinking of all the ways his brethren liked to kill. Poison was a time-honored tradition. It was right up there next to a long-distance shot. Nothing said "gotcha" like an arrow through the eye from five hundred paces. Then there were saboteurs, the trap setters, and finally the shadow dwellers—people like him who savored the up close and personal kill.

Part of him loved the look of surprise on their faces when his targets realized what had happened. It was an indicator of a job well done, but now he was looking for more. Killing for money seemed so trite when there were so many better reasons to do it. His apprentice ShadowLily had shown him a few things when it came to selecting contracts, and he liked her style.

Punish the wicked, protect the good, and he was still allowed to stab people.

The rain splashed off his leather armor as he crossed the street. His eyes were constantly moving, scanning the roofline, searching the shadows, checking the ground in front of him for any kind of threat. The area seemed clear, but someone would have to have some big balls to strike at him here. Tim and his friends might be gone, but Gaston could hold his own against almost any threat.

Sarah Brennen's shop was across the street. Tim asked Gaston to check in on her from time to time to make sure she wasn't having any problems. Why someone would want to hurt such a delightful woman, Gaston would never know. She'd even helped him pick out a gift for Lucy.

Stepping under the covered awning, Gaston gave the rainwater a few seconds to run off his clothes before stomping his boots and opening the door. Sarah kept a clean shop, and he'd hate for her to have to mop the floor on his account. He closed the door behind him and wiped his boots on the interior mat before stepping farther inside.

As soon as he saw her face, Gaston knew something was wrong. He didn't call out but instead dropped into stealth and rolled to the side. Three arrows punched into the door he'd just closed behind himself. It was a clever play, but they should've fired while he closed the door instead of waiting.

Now he knew where all of them were.

Gaston pulled four throwing knives from the bandolier around his chest. He threw the first blade, and before he heard the *squish*, the assassin was moving. The next blades must've come out of nowhere to the two men who found them sticking out of their chests. Gaston moved through the shop like a ghost.

Nothing could stop him.

"I've seen about enough of that." Liam Ravenstorm appeared next to Sarah with a dagger in his hand. "Come on out before you force me to do something drastic."

Gaston dropped his stealth, pulling the short swords he used in place of daggers free from behind his back. "Drastic would be me sending your head back to mommy in a box."

"You'd let your order crumble to save this bitch." Liam grinned as he drew his dagger tight enough against Sarah's throat that a single bead of blood flowed down her neck. "I knew you were a loser, but this, caring for her, it's more pathetic than I expected."

It didn't take much for him to know it was a trap. What bothered him was he couldn't see what Liam's final play was. The bastard planned this attack well enough he had time to hide whatever trap he hoped to lure Gaston into with magic. Then there was the fact he was Duke Ravenstorm's son. Killing him could be the very thing that pushed the nobility over the edge and wiped out the assassin's guild for good.

Not killing him instantly was the hardest thing he'd ever done.

"It's always all talk with you Ravenstorms." Gaston sparked his daggers off one another. "Never have the guts to pick up the sword yourself."

If he could keep Sarah alive as a witness that Liam attacked first, maybe there was a way he could kill the prick without castrating his order in the process.

Liam bristled. "I have a blade in my hand right now. Go ahead and take a swing."

"Takes a big man to hold a knife on an unarmed woman." Gaston let out a peal of condescending laughter. "It's kinda sad you don't have the balls to tango."

"We'll have our day to dance, big man, but as it is, Mother would like to see you first." Liam pulled Sarah tightly against him. "I'm sure your brother would be delighted for the company."

"Noooooo!" Sarah wailed as she struggled to pull away.

Liam shoved her to the floor with a cruel gleam in his eyes. "So what say you, assassin? Will you come with me to save her life, or will she die here for nothing?"

There was nothing he'd rather do than kill the smug little prick, but it simply wasn't in the cards at the moment. Tim asked him to protect Sarah, which he would do even if it cost him everything.

Gaston slid his short swords back into the sheaths on his back. "Let's get this over with."

He felt a man step up behind him, and his vision went black.

Lucy felt ecstatic as she walked in the front door.

There was a chance she wouldn't have to marry that idiot Liam to bail her father out after all. If there was ever a group of people she felt safe trusting her fate to, it was Tim and his band of adventurers. There was no way they would let her down. They would win or die trying.

Desmond's word wouldn't have been enough for her a few weeks ago, but after the death of his mother and the king's return to health, the prince seemed like a different man. There was a pep to his step that had been lacking before. The once dour prince was finally coming into his own when the kingdom needed him the most.

Yet she would take Prince Desmond at his worst as a ruler before she would kneel to the duke.

Was it possible there could be a civil war? If there was, Lucy knew which side she would be fighting on, and it wouldn't be as a Ravenstorm's pawn. Her thoughts drifted to a dark place, and she shoved them away.

She was in love. It was better to focus on that.

Gaston wasn't the kind of man she ever thought she'd be interested in. He was of low birth, not religious, and certainly had a reputation when it came to the ladies, but there was a roguishness about him that delighted her. That and the big tree trunk-sized arms. Lucy thanked Eternia a million times over for the man's body. It was hard as a rock from the neck down, and when pressed against her, it felt like heaven.

The first time they'd been together, it was a rash mistake made in the heat of the moment. There was nothing like a good fight to get the blood pumping, and they'd been in a bit of a pickle. That was months ago. Now she couldn't imagine her life without the burly brute. He might not be perfect, but Gaston was devoted to her in every way that mattered.

And she to him.

As Lucy put a cap on her sour thoughts, Reginald walked into the entryway with a look that almost stopped her heart.

"We have a guest," her servant and bodyguard said dryly.

Lucy looked down at her rumpled dress and plucked at her messy hair. "Please tell them I will be in momentarily. I need a moment to collect myself."

Stepping into the hallway, Duke Ravenstorm eyed her like a piece of beef. "I don't see what all the fuss is about."

"Yes, I can see how it would be hard for you to understand working for a living when it's so much easier to bribe, cheat, and kill your way to the top." Lucy might be marrying her son, but she'd be damned if she let this bitch shame her for making an honest living.

Everything she'd built she'd done without family money, from the ground up. The hard way—how you were supposed to do it. Not only that, but she'd spent a considerable amount of her fortune bailing her father out of hot water the first time his gambling got the better of him. Thankfully she had a way out of this disaster. The duke might not like the outcome, though.

"Don't forget fucking." The duke clucked. "Men do all sorts of unreasonable things to get inside a lady. Then they'll do so much more to keep anyone from finding out about it."

Walking forward, the duke smiled warmly. "Like your father and his luck at the tables. He borrowed so much to keep up appearances. Now you'll pay them off in much the same way I had to."

Not bloody likely.

"Is there something I can help you with? As you can see, I'm in a bit of a state and would like to get cleaned up." Lucy was starting to wish she'd used the servant's entrance.

The duke breezed past her. "Of course, dear, and when you finish, I'll have a carriage waiting to escort you to my estate. You see, I can't have you getting cold feet before your big day."

"If you think I'm going to wait under lock and key to marry Liam, you are greatly mistaken." Lucy kept her voice flat and in control.

The duke opened the front door and turned to face Lucy with a sneer that almost peeled the paint from the walls. "You can get in the carriage, or I will bankrupt your father. You see, dear, when you hold all the cards, you can do whatever the fuck you want."

The duke gave her one last haughty look before walking out the front door. The bitch even left it open just to rub it in.

Reginald ran to the door and shut it before sliding every latch and lock in place.

"That was the worst morning of my life." Reginald sagged against the door and slid to the floor in exhaustion.

Lucy pushed her emotions down. She knew something like this might happen. She simply hadn't expected it so soon. All of her hopes now rested with the Blue Dagger Society and their quest to end the Sisters of Eternal Bliss. If they could pull it off, she'd marry her love, and if they couldn't, the toad Liam.

She reached out and helped Reginald to his feet. "There's been a development. I think we're going to be fine."

"Tell me everything." Reginald sounded as hungry for gossip as one of the girls on the kitchen staff.

Lucy pulled him toward the stairs. "Draw me a bath, and for the love of Eternia, have someone fetch me a bottle of wine." She paused, savoring the moment. "Then, my dear Reginald, I'll tell you everything."

"Wine!" Reginald screamed as he bounded up the stairs toward the bathroom.

Lucy laughed at his antics and followed him with a good deal more dignity than most people doing the walk of shame and caught by their soon-to-be mother-in-law.

CHAPTER TEN

"I hate when we don't get any loot." Cassie spat on the ground as she marched away from the field.

JaKobi chased her, but Tim turned to smile at his girlfriend. "It wasn't all bad. Ten gold and we had thirty people added to our side quest."

They were almost there, a few more people, and they'd earn the bonus.

ShadowLily gave Tim a quick kiss before grabbing his hand and dragging him toward the exit. "Should be pretty easy for us to round up the last people."

Lorelei was walking behind them. "Do you think we should try to free over one hundred?"

Tim stopped walking as his brain kicked into action. The real question wasn't if they should keep freeing people. It was whether continuing to release them would provide their group with any additional benefit. If the antidote was as cheap and easy to make as Ernie said, there wasn't a reason to hold back. If they died for some reason, Tim would order another batch of the potion for Ernie to make before they came back.

"I say we free as many people as we can, but let's not go out of our way to look for side quests." Tim's feet started moving again.

Lorelei pointed ahead at JaKobi, who was kneeling in the dirt, rubbing the earth through his fingers. "What do you think he's doing?"

"Probably trying to figure out how to light dirt on fire." ShadowLily picked up the pace. "Let's hurry before he hurts himself."

When the trio grew closer, the ember wizard looked up at them with hopeful eyes. "Do you think they have a farming simulator? I love growing things."

Tim helped his best friend up. "Simulator, no, but you could always buy a farm and grow whatever you want."

"That sounds awesome." JaKobi's hands burst into flame, cleaning off any residual dirt. "You know, after we're done saving the world."

Tim gave him a high five. "Time to catch up with Cassie."

The four of them hurried to catch the tank already waiting by the main trail. It didn't take a genius to see Cassie was ill at ease, but after such a resounding victory, her mood seemed out of place. This was about more than loot, and they needed to get to the bottom of it before they continued.

Moving next to Cassie, Tim got her attention by gently nudging his shoulder into hers. "What up, girl?"

"Those people were getting fed to a giant bug, and they had no idea." Cassie kept her eyes focused off in the distance. "Just seems kinda sad, you know?"

JaKobi moved up on the other side of her. "It would've kept going on if we didn't put an end to it."

"We turned that fucker into bug paste." Lorelei smashed her hands together.

ShadowLily laughed. "Like the opening of MIB, sometimes you're the windshield, and sometimes you're the bug."

"At least this one was wearing a stump instead of an Edgar

suit." Cassie huffed. "Let's go track these sisters down and put an end to this."

She walked down the path, and the rest of them fell into their normal battle formation. There hadn't been a lot of trash yet, but that didn't mean packs of baddies weren't about to jump out at any moment. Tim checked to make sure none of them were suffering from any detrimental effects and their health was full.

Once Tim was satisfied, he kept his eyes up, ready for anything.

They followed the path past the farm and fields and into the woods toward the sisters' cabins.

Since they cleared out the farm, they hadn't seen another person on the property. Now that the sisters knew they were coming for them, they found a way to hide the rest of the people the group needed to cure. Tim knew they would have an opportunity to save more of the sisters' victims at some point. No one in their party had ever received a quest they couldn't complete. So it was a matter of putting in the effort to find them and if the hassle was worth more than ten gold.

There was a sense of calm as they walked down the quiet path. Something about being surrounded by trees and nature without the city's noise put him at ease. It helped that they hadn't faced a single pack of trash mobs since entering the place. A bird chirped and Tim looked out into the forest, feeling a little of his serenity vanish as he scanned the empty rows of trees.

Was it a signal?

The fact it had been an hour since they faced Stumpy and they hadn't seen or heard another living thing except the bird stood out as odd to him. Why the big lull between fights? The first boss they faced had come out of nowhere. Were they in for another fight that started out of the blue? Now that Tim was thinking about traps and boss encounters, he couldn't think of anything else, and the little tranquility he'd been holding onto vanished.

Instead, his eyes roved across the forest, looking for new threats.

Cassie passed ShadowLily a coin. "I thought he'd crack sooner."

"I told you, my man is getting less paranoid by the day." ShadowLily winked at him and slid the gold into her pocket.

Did they really bet on how long it would take him to freak out if nothing happened? He didn't know whether to be insulted that Cassie thought so little of him or happy his girlfriend bet on him to win. In the end, it didn't matter. They were both right. He was a total mess when something unexpected was on the horizon. Tim liked to have an idea of what was coming so he could build a plan with plenty of redundancies.

The way stations they passed along the trail were still stocked with food, drinks, and flowers to smoke. Even knowing that a single bite would enslave him, it was hard not to feel the lure of temptation. *It really was good stuff.* Walking past the rows of delicious food he couldn't eat reminded Tim of being on a diet, or like when he walked past Joe's and felt the call of their famous buttermilk pancakes. He knew it was wrong, but pancakes covered in butter and dark maple syrup always felt so right, even on a diet.

God, he ate like a man twice his size and loved every second of it.

At least now that he was eating virtually he didn't have to worry about working off the calories. The worst part about splurging was always paying back the calories at the gym or with salad. There wasn't a thing in the world that made him think about what he was eating more than seeing how few calories he burned on the elliptical.

At least the elliptical wasn't running.

"You're drifting." ShadowLily nudged his shoulder with hers.

Tim snapped out of his thoughts and focused on her. "Sorry, it's so damned empty out here."

"Don't worry, guys, the wait is almost over." Cassie had her staff out, and her focus was locked onto a white robe glimmering through the trees ahead of them.

They walked around one final bend in the trail and emerged into an open courtyard. The trees continued as far as he could see, surrounding a small village of white-robed women. Their houses were simply huts with plastered walls and thatched roofs. In the center of the open space was a giant totem with flowers leaning against the base as offerings.

How had Tim not known this was here the last time he visited? Was this a trick, or were the women and village really here? He had the distinct feeling as his team moved closer that they were crawling into the belly of the beast instead of fighting their way out of it. It was like they walked into the village from *Midsommar*, except everyone was female. The women sang as they worked, completely ignoring the group until a young girl laying flowers at the totem's base of the totem pole saw them. She shrieked and ran back toward the protective arms of the others.

An older woman dressed entirely in black moved out of the sea of white robes. Some of the women knelt as she passed. This was the village elder and someone who expected respect. Then he noticed a difference in the other women's movements. It wasn't only respect they showed. They were almost afraid to touch her, some cringing away in fear.

Fear was a great motivator, but eventually, the fearful rebelled.

The flowers at the base of the ancient totem burst into bright blue flames, and the woman walked toward them without a care in the world. Her gaze stayed fixed on a point on the horizon, her lips murmuring a prayer only she could hear. A single cry escaped her lips as she stepped into the flames, and she was gone.

"What in the fuck did we just see?" Lorelei looked at the remaining villagers. They were already returning to their chores as if nothing out of place had occurred.

JaKobi tugged on Cassie's sleeve. "Hey, guys." He sounded worried.

Tim looked up and saw the shimmering veil that indicated the start of a boss fight filtering down around them like a dome. If they wanted to get out, it had to be now. Otherwise, the battle was about to start.

"Everybody ready?" Tim called.

Cassie snorted. "I didn't come here for the brownies."

The dome around the courtyard sealed them inside with the totem. Now that they were trapped, the carvings on the totem pole glowed with power. Light flashed from the glyphs, brighter and brighter until they couldn't see anything. Tim had his eyes closed and his forearm across them, and it was still too bright.

Then the glyphs extinguished, and his eyes were still swimming with light.

Tim blinked rapidly, trying to get his eyes to adjust to the normal daylight again. When they finally focused on what was in front of them, he wished he was still blind. How in the hell had such a tiny woman gone into the flames and come out as a giant monster?

Cassie whipped her staff around in a way that would've made Bruce Lee jealous and charged at the demon as if it were the last pair of shoes in her size at a clearance sale.

Covered in fire from head to foot and carrying a sword and

whip, the Balor demon roared. Two massive wings flapped, sending a blast of flames straight at the group. Cassie rolled out of the way as the giant demon curled in its wings and lashed out with its whip.

Tim had seen enough. He cast Curse of Giving and Hex of the Shattered Beast. With his initial volley of healing out of the way, it was time for a trio of Healing Orb and Behold My Power. While it paid to save his hardest-hitting damage spell for the end of fights, sometimes it was nice to get it out of the way early. The extra damage Behold My Power dealt to the group at the end of the current fights made the spell harder to use.

A fireball broke against the demon's swords, splashing it with fire, and all it did was laugh.

"Unexpected." JaKobi cast his Sunbeam spell, and a smile spread across his lips as the damage done was more to his liking.

Tim turned away from the ember wizard and scanned the battlegrounds as he cast a quick Curse of Sacrifice to boost Cassie's health.

The women dressed in white lined the far end of the courtyard. They were singing, and their hands were intertwined. They rocked back and forth as they watched the battle, almost as if in a trance.

I don't want to be The Wicker Man.

Lorelei was leading the show. Her spirit damage was doing wonders for their numbers on the DPS front. ShadowLily was having one hell of a time staying close enough to the boss to do significant damage. When fire covered the boss, it made things more difficult for them. The one thing that would make this fight easier was if there was a way to extinguish the flames.

None of them had an affinity for water, so they had to grind him down the old-fashioned way.

Tim quickly found out that no one was safe from taking

damage. The Balor demon used its long whip to lash at the people in the back of the group while keeping Cassie at bay with its sword. ShadowLily was constantly taking damage from the tail or a wing, and he started to think this might simply be a fight of endurance.

Behold My Power hit, and the boss was down to ninety percent health. The glyphs on the totem pole glowed again, and Tim used Disturbance to interrupt whatever was happening. He wasn't sure if it was the right call or not, but the glow faded, and the fight continued as if nothing happened until his Golden Retriever slammed into the demon and burst out of its back. For a moment, only the tiniest glimpse, Tim could've sworn he saw the woman in black inside the demon controlling it.

"Last thing I need is to be fighting a fucking Power Ranger," Tim growled as Cassie took a big hit.

Tim quickly recast his heals and tried to figure out what part the totem pole played in all of this. Was it a gateway, or did she promise her soul to the demon for a certain amount of control? The talisman itself wouldn't be there if it weren't important. He had to figure out what the trick was.

"JaKobi, see if you can light the totem pole on fire." Tim cast Curse of Sacrifice. "If the glyphs light up, use your interrupt."

A brilliant flaming phoenix smashed into the totem a moment later.

"Bro, it's changing colors," JaKobi called, unsure of what to do.

Tim reapplied his Healing Orb and Curse of Giving before turning to look at the totem. The glyphs on the surface were changing colors quickly, but they were going in a sequence. Green, blue, red, white. There was a pattern to it, almost like a slot machine. The question was which color was the totem going to pick, and how bad was it going to fuck them over?

"Interrupt it." Tim made the call to the group.

It was their only chance.

The glyphs flashed faster and stopped on blue. With a flash of brilliant turquoise light, a force pushed their group back to the edge of the area. The Balor demon's fire sucked back into the totem, and eventually only the woman in black remained. The sisters' leader glared daggers at the adventurers as water flowed from the totem pole. Soon the woman disappeared in a mass of swirling magical liquid.

When the magic faded, a giant alligator with scales of electric blue was in front of them. The massive beast was easily forty feet long from snout to tail, and its eyes burned with the same intensity of the woman in black. A wave of magical water grew in front of it, and a single nudge of the creature's tail sent the deadly wall rushing toward them.

Cassie grabbed JaKobi, tossed him over one shoulder, and sprinted to the side. This was like any other movement segment, but this time they were dodging water instead of fire or pure magic. Tim didn't doubt that if any of them got carried away, it was a one-way trip to visit their caseworker, so he ran like the devil himself was nipping at his heels.

They made it around the first wave with plenty of time to spare and ran to the exact opposite side of the map to avoid the next one. They would be fine if they could keep up the pace.

Then his feet hit the mud left behind from the first wave, and a debuff appeared.

Sticky Conditions: movement speed reduced by ten percent.

"Time to light a match." Cassie flipped JaKobi around on her shoulders so he faced forward and slapped his ass.

The ember wizard squawked, and flame erupted from his hands, drying out the ground in front of them as they continued sprinting.

The rest of the group got on the path JaKobi created and continued to dodge the waves until they reached the boss.

Cassie tossed JaKobi off her shoulders so he would land on his feet and pulled her staff free with the same smooth motion. As soon as the tank hit the boss, the fight started again in earnest.

The woman in black was at seventy-five percent health and dropping as Tim recast his heals. For the moment, he was content casting Curse of Sacrifice on repeat. The spell did enough damage to make up for the losses JaKobi was suffering. It was rough luck that the first element they faced was fire, and the second was water. If the totem landed on earth or air, the ember wizard probably would've been on top of the DPS chart.

So far the battle was one of pure attrition. They had two players doing less than optimal DPS with ShadowLily also having to contend with fire, and no massive jaws and a tail. As Tim watched Cassie tangle with the giant alligator, he wondered if their best bet might not be to trigger the totem again and hope for a better result. If they went back to fire or stayed on water they wouldn't be any better off, and he didn't know if there was a limit on how many times they could force a switch.

For now, he went into a mainly defensive rotation, trying to save as much of his mana as possible. The longer a fight lasted, the more he had to conserve his power. The increased regeneration he received wasn't enough that casting was as cheap as he'd like it to be. His mana pool was sitting around seventy percent, and he wanted to keep it there until the next phase change.

Ripples formed on the alligator's scales, and it stomped its front paws. Before the boss' jaws could open, Cassie cast her interrupt. Whatever special attack was supposed to happen didn't go off, but they also lost an interrupt to use on the totem in the process.

It was probably worth it.

They were three interrupts down now, and they only had two left unless one of the DPS had an extra they hadn't spoken about yet. They only had two tries to get this right, one if they needed to interrupt another attack. Things were about to get interesting.

Lorelei darted forward, dashing to the side faster than Tim's eyes could track. Arrows flew from her bow as she darted around in a way that would've made Legolas jealous. Her final attack hit the boss in the eye, dropping its health below fifty percent. The totem pole flashed again, and this time the glyphs were moving slowly. Tim followed the pattern for a moment, then called for the interrupt.

The seconds seemed to last for eternity as the colors of the glyphs flashed slower and slower. His heart was hammering. Blue, red, green, white. Slower and slower. White, *almost there.* Blue, *please go a little faster.* Red. Tim's stomach clenched as a slight shade of green flickered at the top of the glyphs. Would it be enough?

The totem pole flashed green and swept them to the end of the courtyard.

"What do you think green is?" ShadowLily asked as she watched the water suck back into the pole.

Lorelei's lips quirked into a smile. "Giant cannabis monster."

"I'm with her." JaKobi laughed as he thought about the brownies.

Tim couldn't help but chuckle at the thought of it, but he felt like the game was a little too serious to have a giant pot monster attack them. That would happen in a game with a few more humorous catchphrases—*Duke Nukem* or *Borderlands*, but certainly not in *The Etheric Coast.*

ShadowLily pointed as a green mist poured out of the totem, enveloping the woman in black. "I'm pretty sure a giant pot plant is off the table, but it could be named Seymour."

Tim loved his friends, but sometimes comedy required

sacrifices. When the opportunity presented itself, he had to take it. "See more bu—"

"Don't even finish that sentence," ShadowLily said smugly. "You only get to see one butt."

JaKobi looked confused. "Do fly traps even have butts?"

"Just light shit on fire, and let us handle the butt situation." Tim directed his attention to the giant tree monster waiting for them.

Cassie charged across the courtyard, and the boss buried its fingers in the ground.

Cracks erupted in the earth and raced toward the players, tearing up huge chunks as roots lashed out.

Tim did what he did best and threw his body to the side without a thought of anything other than getting the fuck out of the way and don't die. He hit the ground hard and was checking his user interface as he rose to his feet. Cassie had been hit, but she was the tank so she played through the damage. A quick trio of Healing Orb placed Rejuvenate on everyone. Then he ran to catch up with the rest of the group as they sprinted toward the boss.

Things felt frantic as two vines erupted from the ground and slammed back to the earth at random intervals. The entire group was taking damage, but nothing was a knockout blow. Before things could spiral out of control, Cassie reached the boss, and the fight started in earnest again.

As soon as Cassie hit the boss, the earth stopped shaking, but the two large vines stayed aboveground and continued their relentless assault. They had a couple of choices for what to do—attack them, or ignore them. The vines were targeting two people at a time and doing their best to obliterate them. If they could avoid the mechanic, there was no reason to waste time removing the threat.

There was no reason to think the boss couldn't respawn the fucking things anyway.

Tim sat back and watched the group as they moved and fought. When a vine locked onto him, he noticed a faint outline on the ground of where the attack would land. Moving out of the outline, he kept up his healing. If they were all able to stay on top of dodging, he'd keep the fight going the way it was. If they faltered, he'd make the call to take out the vines.

This time of the fight was his favorite part. The damage done to the group was minimal, giving Tim a chance to watch the others work. Normally he would've kept his eyes moving around the group, but JaKobi was unleashing his inner fury, and it was something spectacular to behold. Streams of fire and light burst from the ember wizard as he tried desperately to make up for his lack of DPS during the first two phases.

Someone should've told the devs that trees and angry wizards don't mix.

JaKobi was trying to win this battle on his own. The boss' health plummeted under his relentless assault. Several spots on the boss pulsed with purple light, indicating attacks would do more damage if they hit there. The tradeoff seemed to be that the boss was also getting enraged. A faint red glow appeared that they needed to deal with.

The lady in black wasn't a big fan of fire.

There was nothing they could do about the soft enrage. They had to keep battling until the boss was dead or the totem activated again. Tim cast Who Needs a Shield and Hex of the Shattered Beast on Cassie as the giant tree crushed her in the grip of one fist and slammed her into the ground repeatedly. The extra defense was enough to keep the tank from being squeezed into a paste or smashed into bits. However, when the boss slammed her to the ground a final time, her health plummeted like a witch tied to the rock of justice after being tossed in a lake.

Tim was by Cassie's side in a second, hauling her back like a combat medic while ShadowLily got the boss' attention. The tank was already pulling out of his grip as the heals took effect. Normally he would've snatched her back, but the boss was chasing his woman around the courtyard, and the only one who could save her was the tank. He kept the heals flowing to the tank, wondering how ShadowLily would survive a hit like Cassie took. Then the mist slayer disappeared.

The boss stopped on the spot and bellowed toward the sky in rage.

JaKobi took advantage of the momentary pause in the action and fired a blast of sunlight into the boss' back. Turning toward the ember wizard, the boss screamed and ran forward to destroy the greatest threat. Cassie cut the boss off and turned it away before it could do any serious damage. With the boss back under control, the group fell into a steady rhythm of destruction.

At twenty percent health, the totem flashed again.

This time the pole was only flashing black and red. Tim hoped black didn't mean dead and instead meant they'd face the woman in black. Red would be the Balor demon again. There was only one way to find out which one it would be.

"Lorelei, you're on totem duty," Tim called as he sent out another trio of Healing Orb.

The spirit archer darted fifteen yards to the right in a blink and fired her interrupt at point-blank range.

The totem pulsed with bright red energy, and the magical object sucked the green mist back into itself.

This time while the group waited there was no relief. The sisters in white threw fireballs at them. Tim didn't fancy finding out what being hit by one felt like, so he kept dodging with the others as the demon reformed in front of them.

Despite being at twenty percent health instead of a hundred, the demon looked smug. It was the kind of look that said "I have something nasty in store for you, and you're not going to like it." There had to be a surprise coming their way, and the demon was right. Tim didn't fucking like it.

"I know we're all watching the great balls of fire, but don't end up like Goose." Tim's attention was so focused on the boss that he almost ate a fireball to the face.

Looking back in the fireball's direction, he saw a woman holding her thumb and index finger about an inch apart, in the classic "so close" gesture.

"Damn, even the runs are salty." Tim dodged the next fireball easily and tried to look out for what was coming from the boss.

The next set of fireballs was different. The women in white rolled them across the ground like bowling balls. Each one left a streak of fire behind it that didn't extinguish. The entire boss area looked like some kind of demented pinstriped suit. The flames didn't lash out or spread. If he put his hand over them, he didn't get burned. At the same time, he knew one false step onto the flame-covered ground would incinerate him with a quick trip to Barbara.

In this case, if he stepped on a crack, it wouldn't be his mother's back in jeopardy.

"Watch the fire!" Tim knew it was a pointless warning, but he made the call anyway.

The Balor demon used its whip to keep Cassie and ShadowLily at bay. JaKobi returned to doing reduced damage leaving most of the burden on Lorelei. The spirit archer seemed up to the challenge as she moved around the courtyard, firing arrows.

A trio of Healing Orb was enough to keep most of the group up and thriving, but ShadowLily and Cassie were a different story. Both of them were taking periodic damage from the demon, and he had to keep healing them constantly. The tank wasn't so bad, but ShadowLily was taking a beating.

"Get in there and end this." Tim's mana plunged to under fifty percent.

The mist slayer got the message and rolled forward, sinking her daggers into the demon's leg even though it burned her arms. Tim cast Hex of the Shattered Beast on her and made sure he refreshed Hydrate. He might have to switch into his Way of the River stance if the damage was too bad, but for now, a microburst of Healing Storm was enough to keep her health out of the danger zone.

When the demon hit ten percent health, fireballs burst from its body and flew in random directions. The group was already busy watching their feet. Now there were also chest-high fireballs looking to take them out. Tim dropped all pretense of watching everyone's health and dropped into his Way of the River stance.

His Golden Retriever exploded out of the boss' back right after the switch.

The spike of damage gave the group a burst of healing, but now all of his single-target damage-dealing abilities were going to heal the entire group. Knowing that all he had to do was let loose was a very freeing feeling. Tim cast every one of his damage-dealing abilities except Flame Burst. Divine Light was hitting harder than any of his other spells so he abandoned the rest and cast the same spell repeatedly.

If there was something to be said about shooting magical beams of light at evil incarnate, it was that it was *cool as fuck*.

Tim almost felt like a good version of Palpatine. A small voice in the back of his head told him to walk forward slowly as he blasted the boss, like a hero in an action movie who knows the fight is almost over. Instead, he kept his feet planted to avoid the fire and hammered the boss with Divine Light.

Cassie's health was becoming a concern. Without the extra protection of Way of the Boulder, she was taking more damage than she was used to. Her health was at forty-five percent, but the boss' health was at two. All they had to do was push a little harder, and the fight would be over.

With a growl, Cassie ran forward, dodging a whiplash and jumping inside a sword strike. Her staff came up in a wicked arc, slamming into the Balor demon's chin with a loud *crack*. ShadowLily circled behind, and as the creature fell, she lifted her daggers high above her head, letting the force of the monster's fall shove the blades through its body.

ShadowLily screamed as her arms burned, but she didn't let go until the demon burst into beautiful golden motes that swirled up into the heavens.

Tim followed the path of the motes back down to his girlfriend and cast a heal. The words to the spell died on his lips as he realized the woman in black remained impaled on the weapons.

The sisters in white let out a collective gasp.

Looking up into ShadowLily's eyes, the woman whispered, "Thank you.' Then she burst into a swirl of silver and gold motes rising gently into the sky.

ShadowLily sat there, too stunned to put her daggers away.

"Did she say thank you?" JaKobi looked confused.

One look from ShadowLily was all he needed to confirm that was exactly what she had said. "Let's go talk to them and find out."

They all turned to look at the women in white, and Cassie cut them off. "First, we get the loot."

CHAPTER ELEVEN

"I love loot." Cassie looked like she'd been transported to her happy place as her hand touched the chest.

As she turned to face the group, Cassie's pants changed to a new pair with really cool silver buckles up the sides. "Finally, a set item. Now I need to find the other pieces."

"Hell yeah, girl!" Lorelei gave the tank a high five as she breezed toward the chest.

The spirit archer broke out in the original JaKobi shuffle as she equipped a new leather chest piece. "Spirit Cuirass of the Righteous. It's a pretty solid upgrade."

"All upgrades are good upgrades." Tim motioned for ShadowLily to go next.

The mist slayer approached the chest slowly, her fingers barely brushing the surface. "Daggers of the Night."

She pulled one of the solid black blades free from its sheath. "Would've been better for me before the last class change, but my man said not to be salty about upgrades. So I'll take it."

"They look cool as fuck." JaKobi moved toward the chest. "Wizard's Hat of Ember Rage."

The ember wizard burst into a dance as he equipped his

new hat. "Increases my damage done per successful attack stacks up to five times."

"Sweet!" Lorelei joined JaKobi doing his famous shuffle.

Tim had to step around the two as they continued their celebration. As he walked toward the chest, he looked up and saw all the sisters watching the group. They must've looked like great fools dancing around, but no one rushed out to challenge them.

So maybe we look like badass fools.

He laid his hand on the chest.

Item Received: Shiri's Orb of Greater Healing

Shiri was a woman of incredible renown, but most people knew her for selflessly healing those too sick to make the journey to the temple. Shiri believed that those in need deserved as much love and caring as those who could make the journey. She made it her life's work to make sure everyone who needed healing received it. The king blessed her with the orb as a gift, and now it falls to you.

+5 Endurance +5 Intelligence +7 Wisdom

Special ability: Serving the Needy

When activated, this special ability will increase all healing done by five percent for ten seconds, and all single-target healing spells will heal two targets.

All the extra healing was going to be awesome. Curse of Sacrifice and Curse of Giving would heal an additional person when this spell was active. The bonus to flat-out healing would also benefit all his AOE spells. The real trick would be timing when to use the item for the greatest effect.

Getting more powerful was a good feeling.

He looked up at the group as the chest faded from view. "Increased stats and a little extra healing."

"Good, I hate almost dying," Cassie grumbled as she took the lead.

Tim laughed. "Try not getting crushed to death and being bounced off the ground like a super bouncy ball."

"We all have our crosses to bear." Cassie delivered the line with a straight face.

He would've burst out laughing if they hadn't reached the women in white. The robed sisters moved deliberately around them, encircling the group. They joined hands and spun around the adventurers, almost as if in celebration. One of the sisters started to sing, then they all did.

"Guys, I don't like this. Feels like we're about to get sent back to start. It's game over, buddy." JaKobi looked around nervously as a magical dome appeared over their heads.

Cassie charged at the circle of women like it was a game of Ring around the Rosie. "I've had about enough of this."

She hit the circle of spinning women and was tossed back into the middle like she'd hit a forcefield. Rising to her feet with a bit of steam coming off her shoulders, Cassie growled. "What the fuck?"

"I'm on Team JaKobi. This is going to suck." ShadowLily slowly backed up toward the center.

Tim pulled JaKobi toward the center of the circle with him. "Stack up backs together."

The ground beneath their feet pulsed with dark energy as a line of black extended from each sister, heading to the circle's center.

"Get ready!" Tim screamed as the black lines met in the middle and swirled.

Slowly the black void spread until it reached the sisters. One by one their voices fell silent, then they collapsed. When the last body hit the ground, the void beneath the adventurers opened and sucked them into a whirling tunnel of darkness.

There was no way to tell how long or far they fell. Being sucked into the void was what he imagined walking through a stargate would feel like. Just as Tim was getting used to the feeling of falling and simultaneously being completely weightless, the ride ended. His legs wobbled a bit as the darkness cleared around them.

They were in a cavern. The glyphs etched in the rocks around them were the same as the totem pole representing the elements. The walls glowed with red, blue, white, and green. Tim could've sat there for hours watching the walls swirl with different light colors, but that wouldn't get them out of here. What they had to do now was find out what brought them here and kill it.

Bosses didn't tend to call you into a meeting to say thank you.

"I didn't like the black whirlpool as much as the waterslides, but it wasn't bad." JaKobi looked flushed with excitement.

ShadowLily didn't look as thrilled about their prospects. "How do we get out?"

"Only way out is through." Cassie moved forward down the cavern.

There was only one way to go.

Cassie led them through the cave and into a wide tunnel. The glyphs glowing along the walls made it as bright as if they were walking in the daylight—funky Technicolored daylight.

They kept moving down the tunnel as it curved in a wide arc to the right. Eventually, the passage widened, and it expanded by volume until they stood in an area the size of an NFL football stadium. The cavern's size wasn't the main attraction, though. It was the giant eye in the center of the room.

"The Eye of Sauron." Lorelei let the words out in a single rush of nervous breath.

Tim looked at the eye and realized it wasn't floating. It hung from tendrils of energy that held it in place. Across the cavern's domed top, images played out like they were in the chamber of the precogs. Some of the images followed the sisters. Others covered various areas of the sisters' property and beyond. The eye was controlling them all, or at the very least influencing their actions.

Did this thing get control of his thoughts and actions when he smoked the flower? The idea of this creature being inside his head made Tim feel dirty. *No one gets to control me, but fucking me.* Hatred flared deep inside him. He felt ready to open an economy-sized can of whoop-ass on the boss.

Cassie moved slowly, keeping her gaze attached to the massive eye. So far the creature hadn't paid any attention to them so she crept forward, hoping to get into position before drawing the boss' attention. The tension was mounting as they all waited for the eye to spin around.

When the tank was almost directly below the eye, it spun and focused its glare on her. "Have you come to serve?"

"Do I look like I'm good at kneeling?" Cassie spat back.

The eye jiggled up and down in what must have been laughter. "All will kneel before me. All will be blessed to serve."

"Get the hint, bro. My girl isn't the kind to grovel." JaKobi's hand burst into flames as he eyed the boss.

The eye did its jiggle again. "All will bow before the will of Krathos. I am the sun, and the moon, the eater of worlds."

"Funny how we strolled right up on such an all-powerful being. Maybe your mojo isn't what it used to be." ShadowLily spun her daggers in a quick circle before dropping into stealth.

The eye pulsed with red energy. "I needed to sacrifice some of my drones so I could draw you here. Now I will feast upon you and add your power to mine."

"That doesn't sound very appetizing. I'm a bit chewy myself." Tim patted his robes. "And much too cute to eat if I might add."

ShadowLily laughed. "He is awfully cute."

Speaking gave away her position, but Tim didn't doubt she'd moved afterward.

"Enough," Krathos bellowed. "Snacks are not supposed to

speak." Laughter filled the room, and a bolt of lightning shot from one of the tendrils, striking the ground in the middle of the group.

"Time to rock and roll." Cassie charged forward, using her staff to grab Krathos' attention.

Tim jumped into the battle and immediately cast Curse of Giving and Hex of the Shattered Beast, then sat back to study the fight's mechanics. Bolts of lightning rained down around them. So far they hadn't hit any of the group, but the constant movement slowed down their DPS. His mental clock already screamed they were behind the curve, but he tried to ignore it and looked around for a hint about what was coming next.

Nothing caught Tim's attention as he dodged another blast of lightning. The eye and the images playing across the top of the domed ceiling were the only things here. He looked up, trying to see if there was something among the tendrils holding the eye aloft they could hit for a bonus.

Holy shit, why weren't they trying to attack the tendrils themselves?

"Guys, cut the cord." Tim made the call as he tossed out a trio of Healing Orb.

JaKobi, Lorelei, and ShadowLily all hit different tendrils.

"Try working left to right unless something changes." Tim turned to the left and fired Curse of Giving and Curse of Sacrifice.

A blast of pure sunlight tore through the first tendon, and a blast of magical feedback from the eye hit them.

Tim staggered.

His feet and legs still worked, but if he didn't want to fall, he had to take itty-bitty baby steps, like the first time he hit the beer bong in college. *They should warn people about those things.* On the plus side, unlike the beer bong's effects, here he could remove most status effects with a single spell.

Before casting Cleanse, Tim looked at the rest of the group, and they all seemed to be suffering the same effects. The words to Mass Cleanse were on his lips as the first bolts of lightning rained down into the group. His health dropped by twenty-five percent, and the tendrils had already charged for another attack. Mass Cleanse got the group moving at full speed again, but they all took a second round of damage before escaping the third.

Tim activated his newest special ability, Serving the Needy to increase his healing and take advantage of the extra single-target heal. As soon as he felt the tingle of the effect taking hold, he cast a trio of Healing Orb followed by Curse of Sacrifice to give Cassie a boost. A small blast of Healing Storm brought the group's health most of the way back to full when the next tendon broke.

He was ready for the stagger effect this time, and Mass Cleanse went off almost as soon as Tim took his first wobbling step. The lightning was already coming toward him, and since it seemed unavoidable, he kept his eyes scanning the room for some kind of shielding. The lighting crashed into him, and it didn't feel worth it.

There had to be something they could do to avoid the big damage spikes.

Three more rounds of Healing Orb went out, and a small blast of Healing Storm before the next tendon snapped. His health wasn't in a great place yet, and his mana was doing even worse. The boss dipped under eighty-five percent health though, so at least the group was making legitimate progress.

Tim cast Mass Cleanse. "Slow it down a bit, guys. I'm getting hammered here."

"Damage back on the eye," ShadowLily called as she switched targets. "You tell us when you're ready."

It didn't take long to get them back to full health. By the time the boss dipped under eighty percent health, Tim felt pretty confident again despite his drained mana pool. Now that they knew the basics of the fight the group would take less damage going forward. Still, he needed to make sure he was set up for success if the phase change rocked their world. He activated his ability to double his mana regeneration and focused on dodging lightning strikes as the rest of the group did the heavy lifting.

When the boss hit seventy-seven percent health, Tim made the call. "Tendons."

ShadowLily stayed on the boss as the ranged players targeted the tendons. Five seconds later, a tendon snapped and hit them with a stagger. Before Tim could cast Mass Cleanse, their group was swept to the side of the cavern farthest away from the eye. The ground shook, and fissures appeared. Bursts of bright blue flames randomly popped up around the room with no discernible pattern.

"Too bad this isn't the fire swamp." Tim would've loved the popping sounds so he knew when to move his feet.

He cast Mass Cleanse, clearing the stagger effect from the group as the eye slowly turned back to them. "This time, let's target right to left." He didn't know why but it felt right cutting off the eye's supports on both ends first.

Lorelei smiled. "Remember you're in charge of the calls. When one goes down, we'll flip back to the boss until you give the word."

Krathos was at seventy-three percent health as the barrier holding them back faded. The phase change saved them from the last round of lightning, but the run back to the boss wasn't a free ride. Flames roared from a fissure directly in front of them.

As the flames faded, Tim roared, "Run."

The group took off at a full sprint. Cassie took a blast of fire, but by the time it was over they'd figured out the tricks to the fissures. An orange glow started before the flames came out. So they kept running, and Tim's eyes never stopped moving from the floor to the ceiling. Death from above and below. He almost felt like he was in the trash compactor from *A New Hope* but without R2-D2 trying to save his ass.

Curse of Giving went back on the boss, and a trio of Healing Orb went out to the group. It felt almost instantaneous, but the first tendon on the right snapped. Tim tried to embrace the pain as the shock coursed through him. Despite having felt it a few times now, it was still almost enough to make him miss the orange glow under his feet.

Tim threw himself to the side but still took half of the blast because of the stagger. He was sitting at just above fifty percent health as Mass Cleanse went out. Most of the group was above seventy-five percent, but if he took another hit, it would be trouble. He managed to cast a small burst of Healing Storm before dodging again.

Everyone was attacking the eye now, but it wasn't efficient DPS, and he was holding the rest of the group back by not contributing more. A quick Curse of Giving on the boss and a Healing Orb on himself and Tim felt confident enough to make the call.

"Switch!" Tim shouted as he prepared to cast Mass Cleanse.

Lorelei bounced from spot to spot, firing three arrows from each location in rapid succession before jolting back to where she started in one single burst of activity. The tendon snapped, and she went straight back to attacking the eye as the stagger took effect.

Mass Cleanse went off right after the stagger, saving everyone from fire damage. The entire group continued to eat the occasional burst of lightning, but it wasn't anything they couldn't handle. Krathos was at sixty-one percent health and falling quickly. The boss' health was declining faster than Tim's mana, and that was how he liked it.

A little faster, and we might have this.

"Switch!" Tim smiled, feeling like they were finally finding a rhythm.

This time it was JaKobi who came forward, launching a beam of pure sunlight from his hand. The ember wizard focused the beam on the tendon, draining his mana but snapping the tendon quickly. Then the tendon behind it snapped and the next one.

Looking embarrassed and scared, JaKobi turned to the group. "I dun fucked up, real bad."

"You can say that again," Cassie shouted as the feedback staggered them.

Tim cast Who Needs a Shield and Mass Cleanse, hoping there was some way they would survive this. The lightning came at them, and the group got swept back to the cavern's far end. Krathos was sitting at forty-nine percent, and now the eye was swinging back and forth from the remaining tendrils like a pendulum.

"Enough of these games!" Krathos bellowed with rage, and the eye shook violently.

The eye pulsed with magical energy, then a shadow appeared against the pupil. Something was clawing its way out from inside. The pupil split down the middle with the slash of a giant blade. The shadow disappeared, and Krathos screamed in triumph as he burst from inside the eye, landing on the ground before them.

Tim wanted to say the boss was a minotaur, but he didn't have a bull's head. The body was right, but the head was that of a mind flayer.

What in the fuck was going on?

Normally mind monsters only had one trick, and they used it to take over a person's mind. It sounded like the worst kind of magic imaginable. Tim couldn't imagine what it would feel like if someone else controlled his body. It would make him feel dirty, like when someone broke into his house. He was also pretty sure mind flayers didn't burst out of giant eyes, but the developers always came up with a twist.

This time they also gave the boss the body of a minotaur with a big sword that Hercules would struggle to pick up. Things had taken a huge unexpected turn, and they had to be ready for more surprises.

"Stay behind Cassie, watch for tricks!" Tim called as they moved to meet Krathos.

Cassie glared over her shoulder at him. "You make it sound like I'm your top ho, and you're trying to put me to work."

"I think we all know who my top ho is." Tim instantly kicked himself.

ShadowLily giggled. "Hey, I represent that comment."

All of the chatter stopped when Cassie met Krathos, her staff against his giant sword. The little tank spent most of her time redirecting the boss' attacks and only absorbed a fraction of the damage each one should've done. She made life easy on him unless the boss landed a critical hit, then she ate way more damage than a traditional tank. It was the only downside of not having a metric shit ton of armor for protection.

ShadowLily was taking control of the DPS during this phase. Her daggers dug into Krathos' unarmored body with ease. Arrows appeared in the boss' limbs and burned away when JaKobi sent his phoenix into the fray.

Krathos was at thirty percent health, and the group was in a good place when it came to taking damage. The random burst of lighting from the deflated eye came at them slower as the magic faded. The extra time between lightning strikes made it easier to dodge the fire coming up from the floor. Without the big hits caused by stagger, Tim could finally contribute a little more offense.

Tim cast Behold My Power, hoping there was enough time left before the next phase change for the spell to take effect. It took hold, and he cast his other heals to keep the group's health up from the spell's feedback. The boss was backing up slowly toward the eye. He'd almost made it underneath the deflated sack when Behold My Power took full effect.

A wave of lighting hit them and dropped all of their health to fifty percent. Tim cast right away to bring their numbers back up, but the boss wasn't done with them yet. As Krathos knelt in front of the eye, the damage he'd caused bursting free instantly repaired itself. The eye scanned the battlefield and locked its gaze on JaKobi.

Tim looked at the ember wizard's status sheet.

Gaze of Krathos: you have fallen under the Gaze of Krathos and will attack the person in your party marked with the symbol of the eater.

Symbol of the eater?

He looked down at his gear and frowned as a multicolored glyph appeared on his armor.

"Hey buddy, please don't burn me alive." Tim waved to get JaKobi's attention, and the bastard threw a fireball at him. "Getting his attention was a bad idea." Tim ran.

Cassie picked up the boss again, and ShadowLily went to work doing her thing. Lorelei decided to take a risk and snap one of the tendons holding the eye in place. The group took a big chunk of damage, but Tim didn't notice. He was running in a circle using the boss as a shield and casting Healing Storm whenever he didn't have to dodge a blast of fire.

It was one thing to be fighting the boss but having his best friend trying to kill him was something else. He hoped JaKobi wouldn't feel too bad if he succeeded. They would all know it wasn't his fault. A monster was controlling him. It could be any of them trying to kill him right now. JaKobi drew the short straw.

The boss was down to fifteen percent when Lorelei snapped another tendon. Krathos instantly dropped to nine percent, and the final push started. They wouldn't have a lot of time to end the fight. Every second was precious now.

Tim made sure Curse of Giving was on the boss, and Hex of the Shattered Beast was on Cassie. At this point in the fight, he'd generally focus on his DPS to bring the battle to a quick resolution, but not with an ember wizard on his ass. So far, he'd managed to stay ahead of his friend's deadly assault, but a blast of fire from the floor forced him to slow down.

Lorelei snapped another tendon from the eye as JaKobi paused to line up his Sunbeam attack on Tim. He didn't know what to do so he froze for a second and ran straight for the boss. Right before hitting Krathos, he activated Quick Feet and jumped.

There was no way to know if it was pure luck or if his plan worked out exactly the way he wanted it to, but Tim sailed over the creature so close they could've kissed. The full force of JaKobi's attack hit Krathos, and Tim landed on the ground rolling.

He stood slowly, dusting off his robes.

The battle was over. Krathos was dead.

CHAPTER TWELVE

The images on the cavern roof faded one at a time.

As the images disappeared, the last tendrils holding the great eye severed, and it fell to the cavern floor. Beautiful golden motes rose as the bloated sack disintegrated. Resting in place of the Great Eye of Krathos was a golden chest.

This was the most fun part of the fights for them. Sure, it was nice winning and advancing their story, but every gamer in the world loved loot. A surge of adrenaline formed when a player opened the chest. It was the same rush a gambler felt when they saw the flop. There was the briefest moment when a player touched the chest where anything was possible, and it was that feeling and the friendships that kept them coming back for more.

Cassie looked up at the top of the cavern as she moved toward the chest. "What do you think we'll find up there when we get out?"

"Hopefully, some grateful bitches. Ones that will give us a ride back to the entrance." Lorelei sashayed past Cassie and placed her hand on the chest.

"Hood of the Restless Spirit. Boosts my spirit archer abilities, nothing to scoff at stats-wise." Lorelei tried on the new hood looking every inch the dashing rebellious archer she was.

Cassie looked over the fine white scrollwork embroidered on the dark leather hood and nodded. "Looks great, now back away so I can get my shinies."

The spirit archer wisely moved a step back so Cassie could claim her share of the loot.

"Ring of the Fallen Duelist." Cassie slipped on her new ring. "Boosts my ability to deflect attacks."

Tim felt a smile spreading on his lips. "That's almost like loot for me. Touch the chest again. See if you can get another one."

"Fuck off," Cassie grumbled. "I don't take shit for damage, and you know it."

Motioning for JaKobi to go next, Tim popped back, "Remember that when you wake up in the waiting room to see your caseworker."

The ember wizard stopped on his way to the chest and wagged his finger at Tim. "If she goes down, we all go down."

"Sounds like a weird sex game." ShadowLily brushed past him on the way to claim her loot. "Like one of those things you pick up at a novelty shop."

Tim laughed. "You mean the business named after a castle?"

"That's the one." ShadowLily laid her hand on the chest and stepped away smiling. "Every girl loves a new pair of earrings."

Moving to stand by the others who'd already received loot, ShadowLily bent to show the new earrings to Cassie. "Increases my movement speed when I'm within ten feet of the enemy."

"That should help with all the rolling and the…" Cassie hit imaginary targets. "Stabby-stabby."

"Yes!" JaKobi screamed triumphantly.

The entire group whirled, looking at the ember wizard in shock.

Tim had focused on his girlfriend so much that he totally missed his buddy's approach to the chest, and his scream almost gave him a heart attack.

Watching his best friend like a beat reporter who didn't know if they were about to get the story of their life or instantly murdered, Tim held out an imaginary microphone. "Tell me more."

"Ain't nobody got time for that." JaKobi chortled. "But I got time for this brand-new staff."

The ember wizard lifted a redwood staff that split at the top, holding a solid orange crystal the size of a softball.

Tim gave his buddy a high five and rested his hand on the chest.

Item Received: Eye of Krathos

Every great thinker needs a little motivation from time to time. Some people need to be scared. Others want to feel validated, while some want to conquer the world. This helm will help you accomplish whatever goal you put your mind to, as long as you don't mind ensnaring a few minds along the way.

Special ability: Gaze of Krathos

Fixing the Eye of Krathos on an enemy has a ten percent chance for that enemy to fall under your control for ten seconds. If you fail to control them, they will be stunned for five seconds. This ability doesn't work on bosses or elite-level monsters.

+3 Endurance +5 Intelligence +7 Wisdom

It was a substantial upgrade stats-wise, and the special ability was nothing to scoff at. Still, he was kind of sad about never maxing out his first upgradable item. The new stats were so good that reaching the final upgrade on his old helm seemed like a waste of time. Maybe when he got back to the inn, he could put it up for sale and help some new adventurer find a healthy upgrade.

Gearing was like its own minigame.

"If you've finished staring off at nothing it's time to go." Cassie led them to a portal that formed beyond the chest.

In a few moments, they'd be back on the surface and finally get to find out what the sisters were like free of Krathos' influence.

Tim took one last look around the cavern, committing the fight to memory before stepping into the portal.

The trip back up was a lot better than the one going down. His legs didn't wobble, and he didn't feel like throwing up. Maybe his body was getting used to magic after being in the game for so long. It took his eyes a few minutes to adjust to the sunlight, but when they did, he was shocked at the transformation of the sisters' little village.

Bright, vibrant colors and beautiful flowers in every shade under the rainbow replaced all the drab colors and black and white of the village. A town that had looked about two steps away from being left to rot now looked like it belonged right in the center of a Swedish spring festival.

It was downright beautiful.

One of the sisters approached. A wreath of flowers crowned her head, and her dress was the purest white. A scan revealed her name to be Sister Frea.

She bowed deeply to the group. "Thank you, brave adventurers, for setting us free of that vile creature's influence."

Tim's Tit for Tat quest updated, placing a checkmark next to the hundred people freed. Ten gold coins and a bar of blessed steel appeared in his inventory.

Tim quickly re-equipped his old helmet, not wanting the sisters to see the eye on the top of his staring back at them so quickly after being set free. "It was our pleasure."

"We are truly in your debt. Are you sure there isn't some boon we can grant you?" Sister Frea looked at them with an expression of hopefulness.

Before Tim could respond, Cassie cut him off. "How about a ride out of here?"

"I have taken the liberty of summoning your carriage." Frea moved her eyes toward Tim.

Cassie smashed her fist up into the air higher than when they beat the boss. "Walking is for suckers."

Tim didn't want to let the moment get away from him so he moved toward Frea to ask her a few questions. "Is the food you grow going to be safe now?"

"Not only will it be free from the abominations' influence, but the fruits and vegetables grown here are also the best in the kingdom." Frea winked. "Don't even get me started on the meat."

This was perfect.

Tim smiled widely. "I have a friend with a restaurant that I would love to introduce to you."

"Please tell me it isn't that guy with all the healing food. He's a nightmare." Frea looked worried that she might have to say yes to something she didn't like.

ShadowLily moved forward. "It's my dad's place called Joe's, right next to the Blue Dagger Inn. You should come by sometime and talk shop."

Looking relieved, Frea responded quickly. "I will send a messenger right away and set up a meeting."

Tim and ShadowLily gave her a small bow as Grant pulled up with the carriage.

The carriage driver jumped down from his seat. "The outcome was never in doubt. I knew you'd be successful from the moment you left."

"He tried to run when we approached him." Frea giggled.

Grant wiped some imaginary dust off his shoulder. "Can you blame a guy?"

The entire group got a chuckle out of that. Tim thought it would be a while before the people of the kingdom started trusting the sisters again, but once the word got out about the eye and people tried the food at Joe's, at least they would know there wasn't an immediate threat.

Plus, he really wanted some more of those brownies.

Frea waved at them and passed them a fresh tray of brownies as they climbed into the carriage. It pulled away. Everyone looked exhausted from their day of adventuring, but Tim felt a new sense of energy coursing through his bones. Not only did they save the day, but they ensured that their friends could get married. He couldn't wait to get back to the inn and tell them the news.

"Double time, my good man!" Tim thumped the top of the carriage. "We have true love we need to save."

Grant didn't respond, but the scenery outside the carriage blurred by. They would be back to the inn soon enough, and the smile on Lady Briarthorn's face would be all the payment Tim needed to feel good about the day. Helping a friend reach their dreams was one of the greatest feelings in the world.

CHAPTER THIRTEEN

The inn was quiet and that was never a good sign.
"Liz, where the hell is everyone? We have news." Tim looked at the spunky little bar manager, expecting a smile.
The look of worry on her face nuked his good vibe.
"I'm not exactly sure." Liz wrung the towel in her hands.
ShadowLily stepped around Tim to wrap Liz in a hug. "It's okay, just tell us what happened."
The inn's manager centered herself. "Gaston went to check in on Sarah Brennen, and Lady Briarthorn headed home. I expected both of them back, but it's been too long."
JaKobi pulled the mug of beer off the tap half-full and chugged it down before setting it aside. "No more beer until the work is done."
Cassie looked at the empty mug longingly but turned and headed for the door. "Nope, now we gotta go save our friends."
"Do you really think something happened to them?" Liz looked at all their faces expectantly.
"Gaston is so..." Liz flexed her arms like a bodybuilder. "And you'd have to be nuts to take on a noble unless you were a bigger noble."

Tim frowned as he looked at ShadowLily. "Great and powerful enemies. Sound like anyone we know?"

"Well, the duke is a real bitch," the mist slayer replied after quickly thinking it over.

Cassie looked angry. "Didn't think she had the lady-balls for something like this. Next, she'll be attacking the king."

"Having saved the king's ass once already, I vote we save it before the disaster this time." JaKobi joined Cassie by the door. "Let's head over and see what's what."

Cracking her neck from side to side, Cassie reached out to open the door. "Let's get ready to rumble."

Lorelei had been oddly silent so far, but her eyes were deadly alert. "If someone hurt them, I'm going to kill that Ravenstorm bitch. No one fucks with true love on my watch."

"Hear, hear, sister." ShadowLily moved to her side. "Let's go kill some shit."

Tim looked from Grant to Liz. "We might not be back for a while, but I'll send you a message when we know they're safe."

"I'm counting on you to bring them back." Liz waved them forward. "Stop wasting time."

Tim joined the rest of the group outside in the gentle rain. They recast their buffs and headed toward Sarah's shop. ShadowLily dropped into stealth to scout ahead, and Lorelei moved to one of the nearby rooftops to ensure no one ambushed them from above.

The spirit archer appeared by their sides a few moments later. "All clear."

"Someone's waiting inside," ShadowLily whispered in Tim's ear.

Holy fuck, that was creepy.

Her ability to sneak up on him even though they were in the same group was uncanny. In most games, when a player was stealthed in a group, the entire group would still see them or at the very least an outline. When ShadowLily went stealth, Tim got nothing, and she used it to her advantage.

Someone waiting inside felt like a trap, but they didn't have a lot of options. As long as whoever it was didn't have a magical bomb strapped to their chest, the group would probably be okay. The only order of business they had left before going into Sarah's shop was to send a message to Desmond and let the prince know they'd been successful in their quest against the sisters.

Tim fired off a quick message and pointed at the door. "Don't wait on me. Let's get this party started."

Moving forward, Cassie grasped the door handle to Sarah's shop and yanked it open. The shimmery border that indicated a boss fight filled the entrance.

A voice drifted from inside. "Finally, you know how fucking boring it is just sitting here waiting for someone to show up?"

Tim shrugged when Cassie looked back for confirmation to enter. "Cat's out of the bag, might as well go in and see what this is all about."

"If he hurt our friends, I'm allowed to break him, right?" Cassie's voice came out in a low growl as she kept her predatory gaze on the man inside Sarah's shop.

Moving forward, Tim dropped his voice so only Cassie could hear him. "Let's see what he has to say first. Then you have my permission to inflict maximum pain."

"I like the sound of that." Cassie sneered and stepped inside the building.

Inside the store, the boss took the chair he'd been sitting on and moved it back behind the counter. "I was starting to think you didn't care about your friends very much."

Tim scanned the boss for information and came up with only his name: Donovan. "We would've been here sooner, but we were previously engaged."

"Interesting turn of phrase." Donovan smiled broadly.

"Since I'm here to ensure a certain engagement meets its necessary conclusion."

Cassie smashed her staff into the floorboards to get the boss' attention. "What does that have to do with Sarah?"

"Above my paygrade, but I'd assume it had something to do with her brother's reluctance to help my employer." Donovan took off his jacket and set it on the counter.

Turning to face the group again, he unbuttoned his shirt sleeves and rolled them up. "Some people need to learn to mind their place."

"Can you believe the balls on this guy?" Lorelei mocked. "Just fucking hit him already."

Tim held up one finger to stall Cassie. "Where are Gaston and Sarah?"

Donovan started to speak, and Tim spoke right over him. "Think about your answer carefully."

"I'd be more concerned about where you are." Donovan reached over his shoulders and pulled two swords from thin air.

The blades glistened with magical energy.

Cassie didn't need anyone to tell her what to do. She charged into battle. "Eat a bag of dicks, you lecherous fuck!"

The tank's staff moved like the wind. It was the perfect weapon for her to have against the two swords. She dodged, rolled, and parried everything coming her way as Tim cast Curse of Giving and Hex of the Shattered Beast.

It didn't take long for ShadowLily to join the mix, but as the mist slayer attacked, Donovan split into two. His clone parried the assault from behind while Donovan kept the tank busy. Tim wasn't exactly sure what to make of the move. It was almost like he mirrored himself to avoid getting hit. If the boss could split into two people, it would make the fight a lot more difficult, and they'd have to watch him closely.

Doubt he's only got the one trick up his sleeves.

Tim cast a trio of Healing Orb as his Golden Retriever burst from Donovon's back. JaKobi was working his Sunbeam attack into the fight, and Lorelei was holding her bow sideways in the tight quarters as she blasted arrows at the boss hard enough they should've gone right through him.

It must be nice to have boss armor.

Donovan didn't look all that worried as the fight progressed. He kept an easy smile on his face. Every few attacks, he blocked some of the damage from the other players by cloning himself. So far all of Tim's spells had gone through so he wasn't too worried about healing. For the most part, this was a defensive battle for the boss, and Tim was worried that would change soon.

It wouldn't be like the duke to leave a man here that she didn't think could get the job done. Granted, all Raventstorm's minions had to do was stall them long enough they couldn't stop the wedding. The joke was going to be on the duke in the end.

They'd earned the absolution of Lady Briarthorn's marriage to Liam, and Tim planned to make sure they damn well stopped the wedding. Right now their biggest worry wasn't the fight. It was whether Sarah and Gaston were still alive.

Tim was about to add this fight to the tank and spank category, but Donovan split into three. Cassie tried to corral them, but two clones broke away and ran at different group members. He cast Who Needs a Shield twice before the clones hit their targets.

The amount of damage dealt to ShadowLily and JaKobi was staggering. Both of them were down to twenty percent health. Without Who Needs a Shield, they probably would've been in the single digits. He dropped into his Way of the River stance, trying to regain his composure. He'd expected the clones to stab them, not to grab the two adventurers and blow up.

Now that his spells were healing the entire group, he cast

Behold My Power. A quick flick of his wrist reapplied Curse of Giving, and he cast Curse of Sacrifice on repeat to keep Cassie's health up. All of his heals were just enough to keep the group moving slowly upward against Behold My Power's feedback.

When the spell hit, the boss faltered for a moment, and JaKobi's and ShadowLily's health shot above eighty percent. Tim flipped back into Way of the Boulder to give Cassie the damage reduction again. A quick trio of Healing Orb went out to keep everyone's health moving in the right direction. Now that things were stable he sat back and watched the fight, looking for any opening they might've missed during the initial conflict.

"What in the fuck was that?" JaKobi sent his flaming phoenix at the boss. "I was under twenty percent health."

And that was with my shield.

"I didn't see a sign to signal the attack was interruptible." Tim turned his attention to the smiling Donovan and noticed that his health was below seventy percent.

So the clones are his boss mechanic?

It seemed like a pretty brutal tactic for the developers to have the boss almost kill two players during each transition. If ShadowLily or JaKobi had taken any more damage, they would've had one foot through the door to visit their caseworker. He'd been in plenty of fights that felt overturned damage-wise, and this was one of them.

The plus side for him as a healer was after the big burst of damage things went right back to normal. Tim rebuilt his mana pool as the battle raged around him. Sarah's shop was taking a beating, and he was pretty sure insurance wasn't a thing in *The Etheric Coast.*

Whatever it took, they'd make it right.

It didn't take too much effort to keep his three Healing Orb spells up and Curse of Giving on the boss, so Tim added a few bursts of Divine Light to help with damage. He kept his eyes on Donovan, waiting for any chance to stop his next devastating attack. The boss' health was at fifty-one percent as he cast Disturbance.

The boss shrugged off the interrupt and grinned as his clones appeared.

This time three of the clones raced out from Donovan. Cassie and Lorelei both got hit before Tim's world exploded in pain. It was hard to describe what it felt like to have someone wrap their arms around you and explode in a burst of magical fire, but it didn't feel fucking good.

In two seconds, he'd gone from full health to sitting on life support.

There wasn't a choice. Tim lifted his staff high in the air and cast Healing Storm. Rain fell on him an instant later, and his health bar climbed as rapidly as his mana bar went down. When he hit fifty percent health, it was time for a trio of Healing Orb and Curse of Giving on the boss.

Knowing that this phase of the fight should be relatively damage-free, Tim felt comfortable letting the rest of their health creep toward full strength by letting Hydration do the heavy lifting. His mana trickled back, and he was starting to feel like he could do more to help with the fight when he noticed Donovan was already down to thirty percent health.

"Stop DPS." Tim made the call, and the group stopped instantly.

JaKobi moved closer to Tim as Cassie kept fighting the boss. "Come on, man, we're about to curb-stomp this guy into oblivion."

"Not with four of us at ten percent health and me with no mana to heal us." Tim gritted his teeth as he counted down in his head.

All fights had a timer. At some point, if the players were still alive and the battle had raged for too long, the boss would become enraged and deal double or triple damage until they were all dead. Tim didn't think they were close to the enrage timer, but if it hit after the transition, how much mana he had left wouldn't matter.

His mana pool edged over seventy-five percent full, and he made the call. "Defensive cooldowns when the clones appear, other than that give him hell!"

This is going to hurt.

Donovan sent four clones at them this time as Tim expected him to. JaKobi, Cassie, and ShadowLily went down, and he felt the cold sensations of two arms wrapping around his waist. When the clone exploded, the pain almost broke his concentration, but they'd come too far for him to succumb to weakness now.

This time Tim cast five rounds of Healing Orb as he rose to his feet. The small burst of healing gave him the strength to lift his staff high into the air and call down the goddess' healing rain. The spell went off without a hitch, and he looked up to scan the battlefield as the rain replenished their health. Donovan was right in front of him, blood dripping from his lips, but he had the same cocksure grin plastered all over his face.

"Say hello to Eternia for me." Donovan's swords came down toward Tim in a deadly arc.

Breaking his spell, Tim turned his staff to deflect the blow. He ducked reflexively as the swords came at his head. Everyone was screaming warnings, but it was Lorelei who saved his ass. He didn't see her coming but felt it when the spirit archer slammed into his side, knocking him out of the way of the deadly attack. The sword went into her arm, and Tim switched into his Way of the Boulder stance to her before she hit the floor with a *thud*.

His health was in tatters, but Tim cast Curse of Sacrifice on repeat, trying to keep Lorelei alive.

Her selfless play saved all their asses. Tim climbed back to his feet and attended the downed spirit archer as Donovan gave his final gasp. The battle had been devastating for such a quick fight. Every single one of them was battered, bruised, and broken. It was a good thing all they needed to do to repair was swap their items into their inventory and back again.

This battle was over, but the fight to save their friends hadn't started yet.

CHAPTER FOURTEEN

You knew there was trouble brewing when Cassie didn't care about the loot.

The shadow dancer moved toward the chest with a quick, determined pace. "Let's get this stuff and get to Lady Briarthorn's."

"Do you really think they are there?" JaKobi didn't look convinced. "My money is on the duke's so she can control the situation."

Lorelei looked around the room. "Can we take on the duke?"

"I think we'll have to, but Lady Briarthorn's house is almost on the way so it won't hurt to swing by." Tim wasn't quite ready to commit to an all-out assault when they hadn't heard back from Prince Desmond.

"New belt." Cassie sounded like she cared about as much as a kid who got broccoli for a snack.

The tank moved through the group and headed for the door. "I'll be waiting outside."

JaKobi ran toward the chest, touched it, and ran back. "Must be raining belts. See you outside."

Lorelei looked at the door for a moment and moved toward the chest. "I'll call Grant and get us a ride." She placed her hand on the chest. "Don't tell JaKobi, but it *is* raining belts."

A smile curved at the corner of Tim's mouth despite their friends being missing and possibly in harm's way. Was this their first boss with a guaranteed loot table? There was only one way to find out. He walked to the chest, but ShadowLily flipped over him and touched it first.

"Four in a row. What are the odds?" ShadowLily moved past Tim toward the door. "Don't stand there thinking. We need to move."

Overthinking something, he felt so attacked.

Tim took a moment to look around the room and noticed that Donovan's jacket was still on the counter. It didn't make sense. When the boss died, everything went up in beautiful golden motes. They didn't leave items behind. It would only take a second to check it out.

Hurrying over to the coat, Tim picked it up and checked the pockets. The inner coat pocket had an envelope in it. Inside was an invitation to the wedding of Lady Briarthorn and Liam Ravenstorm. Maybe they didn't need to waste time going to Lady Briarthorn's house after all.

Tucking the invitation into his inventory, Tim moved to the chest and laid his hand on it.

Item Received: Vindicator's Belt of Healing

Ted "The Vindicator" Roberts was a street brawler who turned his talents to healing after beating a man to death in the ring. Patrons could often find him at the Shaky Lion telling the tale. His favorite line was, "These hands used to destroy, but now they fix what's broken." He spent his days healing the needy and his nights drinking ale and sharing tales of his days fighting down by the docks for fish and loaves of bread.

+2 Endurance +3 Intelligence +5 Wisdom

Turning away from the chest as it disappeared, Tim had another thought. Maybe Desmond didn't know they'd completed their task because he hadn't turned in the quest yet. Before they used the royal seal to get to the duke's house, he should probably warn Desmond they were coming. With a quick thought, he pulled up his quest log and selected the right one.

Quest Complete: Tit for Tat

Prince Desmond is a man of his word. In your inventory, you'll find a sealed royal decree to stop the wedding of Liam Ravenstorm to Lucy Briarthorn. If the wedding has already taken place, the document absolves the marriage entirely. Now get your ass moving. You have a wedding to stop.

Tim ran out the door and jumped into the carriage. "Guys, I've got news."

The carriage moved forward, and Tim filled them in on the details.

Moving through the earl's territory was easy enough.

With the disappearance of Watch Commander Brennen, the men were more than happy to let them through and provide an armed escort to the marquess' lands. It seemed the men under Brennen's command were under no delusions about who had taken their boss. While they wanted payback, the soldiers would never be allowed to attack a noble so they sped along those who could with haste.

The marquess' men let the carriage through the gate when Grant flashed them the royal seal. The earl's soldiers followed them through the lands and kept an eye on the adventurers to ensure their safety. Everything went silky smooth until they reached the gate leading into the duke's territory.

Grant pulled the carriage up short and signaled that they wouldn't be traveling further by tapping on the ceiling.

"All right, guys, Cassie is first. Be ready for an attack." Tim made sure his buffs were in place and got ready to file out of the carriage behind everyone else.

This part of the fight always made him feel like a soldier in an old war movie. It seemed like the men were always running into danger through a very small opening. This was their Normandy. The adventurers lined up like a SWAT team, one hand on the shoulder in front of them.

Cassie kicked open the door and leapt out quickly, expecting an attack. By the time Tim made it out of the carriage, he already knew they weren't going to be in an all-out brawl. Things were quiet, the kind that dominated the battlefield before the soldiers started dying. It wasn't a sound anyone could get used to.

The stillness before death came calling.

The marquess' men were all on edge looking at the closed gate leading to the duke's section of the kingdom. There were men posted in a semicircle behind them, ensuring that if the duke attacked they could mount a proper defense. It also meant Tim's group got stuck between the two opposing sides with Grant and the carriage.

This was one of those situations Cassie was always talking about. Violence was coming, and it was no place for Grant and the horses.

Tim signaled the carriage driver. "I think it's time you head back to the inn."

"I think you're right." Grant tipped his cap. "Call when you need a ride home."

"Don't worry. We've got this. Get back to the inn and stop Liz from pulling out her hair." ShadowLily waved away his concerns.

JaKobi quickly added, "Tell her we're going to need a lot of food and beer." He winked at Grant. "She knows what we like."

"I'll see it done." Grant leapt onto his seat and turned the carriage around. The marquess' men parted, letting him leave without an issue.

Moving out of the gap left by Grant's carriage, a woman marched forward with two men following as the rest of the marquess' men sealed the exit behind her. "Commander Tabitha Valiant. Care to tell me what in the fuck is going on here?"

"Duke's trying to force our friend to marry her son." Cassie looked like she was about to explode. "We have a royal decree from Prince Desmond to stop the ceremony."

Commander Valiant looked as if she'd swallowed something sour. "May I see the decree?"

Tim pulled the sealed document from his inventory and held it out so the woman could see the prince's seal. "I'd prefer to deliver the document intact."

"I'm supposed to take your word for it?" Commander Valiant replied incredulously.

Reaching behind himself, Tim signaled Cassie to get ready in case things went south. "I'm carrying the king's royal seal, bearing a document closed with Prince Desmond's mark, and you dare question my intentions?"

The commander looked shocked, but Tim didn't give her any quarter to retreat. "You will bring your men forward and open the gate. By force if necessary."

There was a one hundred percent chance Tim was overextending any authority the prince had given him. Still, he'd be damned if he'd let Lady Briarthorn suffer the humiliation of a marriage ceremony if they could stop it. Then they'd have to track down their friends, even if they had to take on the duke's entire army.

Commander Valiant snapped to the men behind her, "You

heard the man. Form up and get the hammer." The two men ran off. In a much lower voice, the commander added, "I trust you'll tell the prince about my invaluable assistance."

Tim gave her a slight bow. "It would be my distinct pleasure."

"Now that all the mushy stuff is over, can I introduce myself?" Cassie's voice was low as if she was on the verge of losing control.

ShadowLily smiled. 'Let's go together."

Cassie moved until she was close enough to the gate to smash her staff against it. The end came down on the gate with three rapid *thuds*. There was no way anyone on the other side could've missed the sound.

With a great big grin, she cracked the weapon against the gate one last time. "Honey, I'm home."

A slat opened in the gate, and a man stared out the small hole. "By order of Duke Ravenstorm, the way is closed."

Tim produced the royal seal and the scroll. "We come on direct orders from the crown. Are you willing to risk your lives and honor for the duke? Is your duty not to the kingdom first?"

"The way is closed." The man laughed, and an arrow appeared in his throat.

Lorelei looked at the slat in the gate and back at the group. "Sometimes, you've heard enough."

The opening slammed shut.

"It was worth a try." Tim patted Lorelei on the shoulder and turned to face Commander Valiant. "Commander, please open the gate."

Leaning close, Tabitha confided in him, "I've always wanted to do this." She turned away and screamed, "Hammer time!"

A group of soldiers parted and a giant ram topped with a solid bar of steel shaped into a mallet appeared. The hammerhead must have been nine feet tall, and the ram itself at least thirty feet long. Fifty men ran screaming forward and heaved the giant weapon toward the gate. It wouldn't be long now. Fifty feet until they smashed open the barrier.

Forty.

The gate started to open. The men blocking it dug their heels into the ground, but the hammer kept rolling forward. A lone figure stood in the center of the open gate. He watched the ram bearing down on him and stared at it in haughty defiance as if looks could stop a boulder rolling downhill.

His death was inevitable.

The ram jolted to a stop, the hammer inches from his grinning face. The soldiers rolled the weapon back, revealing the lone figure in the opening. It took a few moments, but when Tim saw his face, he knew without needing to read his nameplate this was Liam Ravenstorm. It wasn't brilliant of Liam to answer the door, not when they had the power to stop his marriage.

Unless he was up to something.

Cassie stormed up to Liam. "So you're the greasy little shit who's standing in the way of Lady Briarthorn's happiness."

The duke's son let the insult roll off him like water on a duck's back. "I think you're misinformed. Lady Briarthorn agreed to marry me. Her father is giving her away at the ceremony."

"Not anymore." Tim held up the prince's decree. "The wedding is off."

Liam looked affronted as if he had no idea something was amiss. "Surely, this must be some sort of mistake. I will escort you to the castle personally, and we'll get this all sorted out."

Motioning for two carriages to be brought forth with his hand, Liam gave them a slight bow. "After you."

Cassie couldn't resist giving Liam a shoulder bump as she went past. "It's just as well. Things would've gone about as well for you as they did for Donovan."

It was easy to see the insult didn't roll off quite so quickly this time, but Liam didn't respond. He simply followed the group inside. As soon as their entire party was on the duke's side of the gates, they snapped shut, trapping them inside. The commander screamed orders on the other side of the gate, but it wouldn't matter if all the duke's men attacked right now.

"Donovan was a friend of mine," Liam snarled. "That bitch Briarthorn wasn't my first choice, but I'll be damned if I'll let some low-class street hustlers tell me my business."

Cassie laughed. It was a low, evil sound. The kind Tim expected to hear only from a supervillain or a werewolf right before it shifted and tore everyone apart. It seemed Cassie's hot button issue was standing in the way of true love, and she was ready to start dropping bodies.

"You think we're scared to be in here with you?" The laughter continued. "Why do you think Desmond sent us? We get shit done. Just ask that guy." Cassie pointed at the dead man with the arrow in his throat.

ShadowLily appeared behind another soldier, scaring him so badly he dropped his spear. "We want our friends back. Make it happen, or get the fuck out of our way."

The soldier ran toward Liam, hoping to get behind the man for protection, but young Ravenstorm had other ideas. Moving with a flash of magic he brought the fleeing soldier down. His fist rose and smashed down through the solid steel cuirass. When he pulled the hand free, it held the soldier's beating heart.

Liam used the blood to draw a few glyphs on his forehead, then tilted his head back and squirted the rest of the blood in his mouth like an overeager kid with a juice box. Covered in blood, Liam rose to his feet, and the guards fell back to their huts and closed the doors behind them. A shimmering dome descended over the area.

There was about to be a boss fight.

CHAPTER FIFTEEN

Liam's skin turned black and split as he grew.
The transformation wasn't painless. Liam screamed at the top of his lungs as his spine *snapped* louder than a steam roller at a bubble wrap factory. When young Ravenstorm's legs broke, it looked like he'd pass out from the pain. Somehow the man kept his wits about him as the bones healed. Magical mist swirled up from the ground, hiding the rest of his transformation from their sight.

When the smoke cleared, Liam was ten feet tall and covered from head to toe in dark crimson armor. The shield in his left hand was bigger than Cassie's, and Ravenstorm's sword was a short, cruel weapon made for thrusting. He smashed the flat of his blade against the raven emblem on the shield and advanced.

"Coming here was a mistake, adventurers," Liam snarled. "I'm going to enjoy killing you, and it will be a nice surprise for Lucy when I escort her to our marriage chamber."

"When I've had my fill of your friend, I'm going to burn down that precious inn of yours." Liam smirked as he bashed the sword against his shield again. "Think of it as a wedding present."

"I don't want to die without any scars." Cassie quoted her favorite Tyler Durdin line and charged at the boss.

Tim grinned. *Fight Club* was the vibe they needed to channel right now. "Keep your eyes up, and let's crack open this tin can."

Cassie was at a stalemate with Liam as they crashed together. Both were built for pure defense so it was like watching grass grow or a five-hour round of golf. Tim cast Curse of Giving, knowing the way things were going that a single spell might be able to keep the tank at full health. If she started taking critical hits, he'd have to revise his strategy.

Hex of the Shattered Beast tumbled from his lips, and his Golden Retriever appeared at Cassie's side. There might not be a lot of damage to return, but he got the feeling they would need all the DPS they could get. Keeping his eyes moving around the room, Tim cast a trio of Healing Orb to get the Hydration effect on everyone. With everyone's health in order and no massive surprises, it was time to get into a DPS rotation.

ShadowLily joined the battle. Her daggers left bright streaks on the crimson armor as Tim launched his first Curse of Sacrifice.

Liam was only down to ninety-five percent health.

"This is going to take forever." Tim launched a blast of Divine Light at Liam, but his health bar didn't move.

JaKobi strode forward, sunlight streaming from his hand as he focused the attack through the boss' shield arm. "Unless the enrage timer is unlimited, we're going to have to figure something out."

Lorelei appeared on top of the gate. "Nothing up here." She fired a few arrows and disappeared.

A breeze ruffled his hair. Then Lorelei was back in her usual spot doing damage. "I'm not sure if there's a trick or if the twist is how big his health bar is."

Turning in a slow circle as he continued casting Curse of Sacrifice, Tim looked at their surroundings. There was the closed guard gate and a small portion of the walls. Unless they could open the gate to let in Commander Valiant's men, that was out. The guard huts were full of angry soldiers, so those were a bust. There was a small fountain in the courtyard, but it didn't look like much. He marked the structure anyway in case they needed to jump in the water to avoid an attack.

Sometimes fountains were fountains, and sometimes they saved your ass.

The only other tactic he could think of was trying to remove a piece of Liam's armor so they could get to the tender bits inside. Tim used Quick Feet to run in a wide circle around the boss, looking for any clue on the armor for a special target. Developers had a way of hiding things like Smaug tried to conceal the missing scale on his belly. With the full circle complete, he didn't learn anything new.

Maybe we need to focus our fire.

He needed a target to test that all of them could reach with ease. It didn't make much sense to go after his sword arm, and the head would be problematic for ShadowLily. There weren't many logical choices left, but they needed to start somewhere.

"Attack the shield arm!" Tim focused on where he wanted the next attack to hit and cast Curse of Giving.

The group pivoted without questioning his tactics. It would've been easy for them to do so. Who in their right mind attacks their opponent's strongest point of defense? If they could knock the shield away or break that arm, it would expose an entire side of the boss he wasn't used to guarding to the battle. It was a gamble, but nothing else was working.

Tim quickly cast Divine Light and pressed his attack with Curse of Sacrifice. Liam's health was barely trickling down. Even with the full press, the boss was at eighty-nine percent. Despite the fact the boss' health was designed to move slowly,

Tim was starting to hear the clock in his head going off. They had to make their move soon, or things would get worse for them at the end of this fight.

ShadowLily scored a critical hit on Liam's wrist guard and widened the gap with her next attack before rolling away. JaKobi and Lorelei both saw the opening and went to work. This wasn't the boss' first rodeo, and he moved to place his shield between the two attackers and the wound on his wrist. The problem for young master Ravenstorm was that shield against the ranged attacks put his wrist right where the mist slayer could hack at it again.

Rolling forward, ShadowLily bought one of her blades up and jammed it into the opening with everything she had.

Liam roared in pain as his shield fell.

The armor on his wrist sealed closed, and he flexed his hand a few times to test it out. The shield *hissed*, and Liam kicked it away from him. A few seconds later the item embedded itself in the ground and a small stream of black mist rose from it.

It must've been the price Liam paid for fixing his arm.

Young Ravenstorm was a better fighter than Tim expected. It wasn't often that bullies at the top fought their own battles, but he gave Cassie everything she could handle. Tim expected the battle to get easier once they got rid of his shield, but if anything, it only made the boss faster since he used the armor plates on his arm to deflect blows instead of the much heavier shield. Getting rid of the protection helped up the damage they were doing, but it wasn't enough.

They needed to make a bold move.

"Go for the helm," Tim called.

If nothing else, bashing Liam around the head should keep him off-balance while Tim tried to come up with their next plan.

The helmet wasn't the most effective strategy for many

reasons, but this was a go-for-broke moment early in the fight. Tim reapplied Curse of Giving, then alternated between Divine Light and Curse of Sacrifice. JaKobi and Lorelei didn't have any problems reaching the helm, but ShadowLily had her work cut out for her. Every third or fourth attack she planted a foot on Liam's plated ass and vaulted high enough to swipe at his helm.

Liam's health was down to eighty-two percent, and he was taking bigger swings with his sword to keep ShadowLily away from his helm. Using her daggers like ice picks, she climbed up the boss' back and yanked at the helmet with one hand as she wrapped the other arm around his throat. The two battled for a moment, and something unexpected happened.

Suddenly, Liam dropped his sword and grabbed Shadow-Lily with both hands. He threw the mist slayer like she weighed almost nothing. She flew across the courtyard and hit the gate so hard the wooden timbers cracked.

Tim dropped into his Way of the River stance and cast Behold My Power. Now that his damage-dealing abilities were healing the entire party, he could keep doing DPS while ShadowLily recovered. Cassie would lose some of her bonuses to defense, but Liam wasn't dealing enough damage for it to matter. He kept up the barrage of Curse of Sacrifice, only stopping once to cast a trio of Healing Orb.

Behold My Power hit, and Liam's helmet popped free like the cork from a bottle of cheap champagne. *All fizzle, no sizzle.* The helmet fell and bounced away. The armor dissolved and stuck to the ground, locked in place with the same black mist as the shield.

The boss' health dropped to seventy-five percent, and he spun around like a whirlwind. The short sword didn't give him the most reach, but it kept the group from mounting an effective attack while the boss regrouped.

Stopping at the far end of the space, Liam knelt, heaving for air. "Guards!"

Soldiers streamed from the two huts, five on each side. Six charged toward the group while the other four dug where Liam's armor pieces dissolved. Tim knew he should've been making a call, but he couldn't take his eyes off the duke's son. He thought he'd imagined the blackened skin, but now that they weren't moving it was clear.

I don't know what dark ritual Liam cast, but it fucked him up.

"Priority on the ones trying to get armor!" Tim finally tore his eyes away from the boss to focus on the fight.

Cassie used her chain to grab one of the guards with Liam's helmet. She yanked him right into ShadowLily's daggers, ending his life in a blink. Lorelei dropped the other man, and now all they had to do was stop the two men trying to reclaim the shield while the six men finished closing the distance to their group.

JaKobi scattered all of the men by raking his beam of sunlight across the courtyard. Two of the guards weren't quick enough and were blown apart by the attack. The others were rolling on the ground, trying to smother their singed leather armor. The attack gave Lorelei enough time to stop the two guards trying to free the shield and for Cassie and ShadowLily to fall on the wounded guards, ending the threat entirely.

The soldiers didn't have very many hit points. They were only supposed to be enough of a distraction for Liam to recover. The boss also gained four percent health back during the encounter so stopping the guards faster next time they emerged would be key. This fight was long enough without the boss gaining back health.

At least Liam didn't get his armor back.

Standing to his full height, Liam tossed his sword on the ground and stripped off his gauntlets. Foot-long claws erupted from between his knuckles. The nails were solid black and looked more like raptor talons than Wolverine. If it weren't for the armor, Liam would've looked more like something from an urban fantasy tale than a fantasy novel.

The claws were going to keep things interesting.

"Maybe you should've let him keep on the helmet." Shadow-Lily grimaced as she looked at the boss.

Cassie snorted. "Lady Briarthorn doesn't know how big a solid us killing her groom-to-be is. She owes us one."

"You have the courage to mock me?" Liam snarled and spread his arms wide, roaring like a bear.

JaKobi laughed like he'd heard the funniest thing in the world. "Doesn't take much courage. You haven't done anything that impressive yet."

Lorelei spun her finger in a circle like someone bored and gently prodding someone else to hurry up. "We've seen the spinny sword thing before."

"But not with such an ugly face." Cassie smashed her staff into the cobbles.

Liam's rage boiled over as his top incisors turned into fangs. "I think it's time I showed you something new."

"If he takes off his pants, I'm going to barf." Cassie didn't wait to see what happened next. She charged into the battle, trying to stop Liam from making his next move.

The tank's staff was perfectly suited for taking on two weapons at once. Liam's claws were no different. Cassie spent her time diverting most of the boss' attacks, her DPS crawling to a complete halt. All that mattered was her doing enough to keep the boss' attention so the rest of them could work.

Tim dropped back into his Way of the Boulder stance and kept his eyes open for the next trick. The boss' increased damage couldn't be the only thing they had to deal with. The timer saying go faster was still wailing in the back of his mind, but how much faster could they go?

"Focus on the leg armor." Tim cast Curse of Giving and Hex of the Shattered Beast.

The group hammered the boss' legs. Tim kept up his spell work as he watched his team do the heavy lifting. The right leg armor came off, and the left. Liam felt them now, and a look of desperation replaced the smug smile on his face. Whatever attacks the boss had in reserve, they would see them soon.

Liam's health was down to sixty-five percent and was picking up pace. There was one more key piece of armor they needed to get rid of. Then they would be able to put the screws to him. It was time for the boss to lose his chest plate.

"Center mass, really let him have it," Tim screamed gleefully.

It felt good knowing they were fighting to save their friend from a man who turned into an actual monster. Once they killed Liam, they would have to move quickly because the duke wouldn't take the news well. Killing Lady Briarthorn in retribution wasn't off the table when all the duke's hopes for the future rested with her son.

Overall, Tim felt like they were making up time but were still a little behind. When Liam's breastplate tore free, he finally felt like they had a chance to make up the earlier DPS loss. ShadowLily didn't waste any time getting to work. Huge chunks of the boss' health came off, but they were getting close to fifty percent health, and it was the right time for something big to happen.

"Guards," Liam roared as he jumped away from the group.

Eight men ran out with heavy shields like they were riot police. They lined up, blocking the group's path to Liam as four others worked to collect the boss' fallen armor.

Lorelei and JaKobi killed two of the guards in the back before the wall of shields was entirely in place, but the other two were working furiously to secure the chest piece. They needed to take out the wall of guards before they could deal with the other two. The entire time, Liam's health ticked up. If he regained his armor on top of that, it would be disastrous.

Cassie couldn't break through the shield wall, so instead of ramming against them pointlessly, she tossed ShadowLily over the top. The mist slayer landed in a roll and came up swinging. Within seconds the mist slayer had their entire formation in shambles so the ranged DPS could pick off the stragglers.

They killed the guards so quickly, but it wasn't fast enough to stop the soldiers from freeing Liam's armor. Thankfully the men didn't have time to start putting it back onto the boss so the adventurers still had time to act. The stack of armor pulsed with crimson light. The glyphs on the plating flared so brightly they had to look away.

Dark mist rose from the armor as it bubbled away to nothing, and Liam started his final shift.

Liam's black skin grew a white patch on his chest. He looked like a furless werewolf now, not the most flattering look. The skin around the boss' head pulled tight, almost like a demon from an old-school horror movie. The only thing he didn't have yet was wings, but Tim wouldn't put it past the devs to have some pop out when they least expected it.

Nothing good happens when you start cutting out hearts.

The ground next to Liam cracked, and his suit of armor rose, standing on its own. Crimson energy pulsed through the cracks in the armor as the suit lifted the sword in a salute. It was almost as if the armor was inviting them to battle. The group was effectively facing two bosses now.

How did you destroy a suit of living armor?

"Dude, where do I get a set of armor that can do that?" JaKobi was looking at the armor in awe.

Lorelei smacked him on the back of the head. "Maybe we can worry about that after we kill him. You know, the guy who's trying to force himself on our friend."

"She agreed to terms!" Liam screamed, his words almost unintelligible as the shape of his mouth changed.

Tim laughed. "You have a lot to learn if you think that coming to terms means a woman is interested in you."

"I'd be damn right insulted if you said that to me, babe." ShadowLily gave him a meaningful look.

Cassie snarled, "You can't purchase a woman's affections. You have to earn them."

"Hopefully by a guy with a better-looking face." Lorelei was watching the Liam demon like it was a ten-foot-tall spider and she had a bad case of arachnophobia.

"What do you know about the handsomeness of men's faces?" JaKobi laughed.

"Enough to see that some," she pointed at the ember wizard, "are better than others." She pointed at Liam.

The suit of armor charged at Cassie as Liam jumped. He was tired of their witty banter and wanted to end their lives posthaste. Tim would've laughed at the absurdity of fighting a demon-like creature and a suit of armor at the same time, but this was a fantasy game with magic, and anything was possible. Young Ravenstorm must have made a pact with Vitaria to be twisted so thoroughly to the darkness.

They needed to put down anyone working with the dark goddess.

Liam landed on Lorelei and ripped into her with his claws. "Tell me I'm not beautiful again, bitch!"

His scream as he tore into her was almost inhuman.

Getting people out of trouble was normally the tank's thing, but Lorelei wasn't going to live long enough for heals if Liam kept up his brutal assault. His claws came down again and again, puncturing the spirit archer repeatedly.

"Do your mist thing," Tim called as he cast Healing Orb.

Lorelei shifted fifteen feet to the side. The only problem was she shifted right next to Tim. "Oh, fuck."

Liam turned toward them with a hungry smile. His tongue darted out between his fangs to lick his lips. Cassie was still grappling with the suit of armor so they weren't going to get help from her anytime soon. All Tim could do was heal the shit out of them and pray for the best.

Leaping high into the air, Liam wore a look of triumph as he descended toward them.

Liam landed next to them and laughed as Tim dragged Lorelei away. "I'm going to enjoy breaking Lucy's will, but you won't live long enough to see it."

The demon Ravenstorm stalked forward for the kill, his steps as steady as an executioner's.

A blast of sunlight hit Liam in the side, forcing him to stagger. The relentless assault continued until the boss dropped to one knee, lifting an arm to shield himself. As soon as his knee hit the ground, ShadowLily snapped back into existence and was on him faster than a New York rat on a scrap of a hotdog bun.

The mist slayer's daggers were dealing huge amounts of damage against Liam's unprotected flesh, but she was also taking hits. Lorelei was stable for the moment, and Tim would have to focus on ShadowLily. Giving twice as good as she got only mattered when their health pools started in the same place. Hers was significantly smaller at eighty percent than Liam's was at twenty.

Tim cast a trio of Healing Orb and cast Curse of Sacrifice on repeat.

Magical energy shot from Liam in shockwaves. Sometimes the bursts were at chest height, and other times they tried to take out the group's ankles. Cassie was still dealing with the armor, and Liam realized fighting the mist slayer was a waste of time—he needed an easier target to pound on.

Liam's eyes locked onto JaKobi, and he leapt into the air.

The ember wizard quipped, "Guess he didn't appreciate the extra sunlight."

The boss was coming down right at his best friend, and Tim didn't know what else he could do to help. His mana was in the shitter, and his brain was frazzled with the non-stop movement and the boss changing targets so quickly. Whatever happened now would determine the fight's outcome. They'd come too far to lose now. They were going to end this.

"Defensive cooldowns!" Tim shouted at the group.

JaKobi moved a hand in front of himself, and his robes flickered with bright blue flames for a moment. Instead of retreating, he fired a new beam of sunlight at Liam as he descended. The attack wasn't enough to redirect the boss when it was coming at the ember wizard like a rocket, but it did rip away another three percent of Liam's health.

The DPS that felt like a win turned into a disaster as Liam hit the ground and eviscerated JaKobi. His claws tore through the ember wizard's robes like they were tissue paper. The shockwaves never stopped erupting from Liam, and now JaKobi was eating every single attack and dealing with the claws.

"Hit the panic button." Tim switched his Way of the Boulder stance from Cassie to JaKobi and blasted the boss with Divine Light and Curse of Sacrifice.

It didn't seem to matter what he did. The best Tim managed to accomplish was a net-zero. JaKobi's health didn't improve no matter how furiously he cast his spells. His mana dipped from precarious levels to damn near non-existent in a flash. He had to slow down his heals, or he'd leave them all defenseless. Things needed to change, and soon.

Tim looked right. Lorelei was getting back to her feet. ShadowLily was nowhere to be seen, which meant she was looking for another moment of opportunity. That only left him to get the boss off his best friend, and he wasn't exactly sure what to do about it.

"This has to be the worst idea I've ever had," Tim whispered as he started running.

Halfway to the boss, he activated Quick Feet and sprinted forward. Turning his shoulder to take the brunt of the impact, Tim crashed into the boss at full speed. It felt like he'd thrown himself into a brick wall, but it was enough to send Liam stumbling away. The boss turned his attention to the healer, but before he could move, ShadowLily appeared in front of him, her daggers ripping into Liam's unprotected stomach.

The daggers slashed, and all Tim could think of was the time he gutted a fish.

The burst of energy from Liam was intensifying now. The damage was unavoidable, and they were all feeling it. All Tim could do was switch into his Way of the River stance so his heals would go out to everyone. Liam's health was under ten percent. All they had to do was last a little longer.

"This is Sparta!" Tim kicked his foot out and hoped everyone still knew that meant it was time to kick ass.

Curse of Sacrifice was his favorite spell for this situation. Each blast returned health to everyone in his party although it took a little of his in the process. Tim kept up the barrage of curses until everyone's health hit fifty percent. Then he threw his arms to the heavens and cast Healing Storm. The rain poured from the sky above them as the fight continued to rage.

Liam was down to five percent health when the suit of armor *crashed* to the cobbled road.

Switching targets, Cassie picked up the boss, and Tim activated Way of the Boulder to increase Cassie's protection. Now that the tank was back in charge, he cut off Healing Storm and applied Curse of Giving to the boss again. A quick trio of Healing Orb took the last of his mana, but it was worth it to see everyone's health back at a stable level and rising.

As Liam's health floundered to three percent, he shrank. The magic was leaving his body now, and soon he would be a naked man lying in the street. The group backed their DPS as the last of the boss' life bled from him.

Walking forward with his staff raised high in the air, JaKobi brought the weapon down, going for the killing blow with a melee strike from his weapon. The staff arced down with deadly purpose, and there was a flash of light.

Tim didn't remember how he started flying, but he would remember how it felt to smash into the gate for the rest of his life. Slowly hauling himself back up, he sent out a heal to everyone and turned to see what had happened. There was a crater in the ground where Liam's body had been as if a meteor had hit there or a bomb had gone off.

Golden swirls of light rose from the hole, and a chest appeared.

CHAPTER SIXTEEN

Still shaken from the blast, Tim cast Healing Storm. Everyone was looking at the crater in the ground, wondering the same damn thing. How did a man explode like that? Maybe it was the magic armor running out of juice or the last attempt of a man who knew they'd defeated him. It didn't matter now. There was a chest in front of them, and they had more important things to worry about than the last two percent of Liam's health.

"That was unexpected." Tim did the inventory trick on his armor to clean it.

ShadowLily stopped wiping the grime from her leather armor and did the same trick. "He went out with a bang."

"Nice one." JaKobi gave her a high five as he crept closer to the crater's edge. "There isn't any blood."

Lorelei looked over the edge. "That shouldn't be possible. Bombs aren't exactly clean slates."

"If it was big enough to erase him, we would all be dead." Cassie peered down into the fifteen-foot-deep hole and let out a low whistle.

Tim looked over the edge for the first time and saw the

gentle slope to the bottom. He knew instantly that his friends were right. This was no normal hole. There wasn't a drop of blood, not a finger, not even a bit of goop.

"The motherfucker pulled a Peter Pettigrew." Tim spat down into the opening and looked at the chest. "So what is this, a trap?"

Cassie grinned. "It might be. Better let me go first."

There was a better than even chance Cassie only wanted the first piece of loot, but if it was a trap, it wasn't worth taking any chances. Tim backed away from the edge so any explosion from the chest wouldn't get him.

"Good luck!" he called over the edge.

"Don't be so dramatic. Everything is fine." Cassie sounded bored.

Tim peered over the edge again. "It is?"

Cassie winked up at Tim. "We'll find out together."

The tank placed her hand on the chest. Tim tensed, but nothing happened. After a second, he loosened up, almost let down by the anticlimax.

Cassie held up a pair of new gloves. "The loot is real, and it's not half bad!"

"If it's not a trap, shouldn't we assume Liam is dead?" JaKobi looked down in the hole again as if this time he would find a body part he missed the first time.

Tim laughed as he moved forward to take his turn at the chest. "You know what happens when you assume?"

"You miss out on the loot." Lorelei laid her hand on the chest. "Earning of Ravenous Intent. Has a fifty-fifty shot of returning one percent of the damage dealt as health, or increasing my damage by one percent for five seconds."

"Damn, that's sweet." ShadowLily set her hand on the chest. "Throwing Knives of Prolonged Exposure. Extends any active poison duration by ten percent."

Tim broke out in the JaKobi shuffle. "That girl is poison."

"Hey man, stop stealing my moves." JaKobi placed his hand on the chest. "Oh, Necklace of the Withering Sun. Adds splash damage to my Sunbeam attack."

Tim gave JaKobi a high five. If they were ever in a position where they had to fight more than one monster at once, splash damage was super helpful. So far it sounded like everyone was getting pretty solid upgrades. Tim's excitement built. There was always a rush when opening a chest, like scraping off the last number on a scratcher. There was always the sense of hope this would be the time he won big.

Everyone was looking at him, and they were right. It was time to get moving, but Tim had to get one thing off his chest first. "JaKobi, when you create something as perfect as the shuffle, people are going to gravitate toward it naturally."

"You can do my dance whenever you want." The ember wizard had a big shit-eating grin on his face as if he'd won a prestigious award.

Cassie groaned. "I'm never going to get him to stop doing it now."

"Stop doing it." ShadowLily started to jam out. "Why would we ever do that?"

Lorelei joined in. "Yeah, that's what I'm talking about."

Turning away from his friend's shenanigans, Tim laid his hand on the chest.

Item Received: Hex Witch's Shoulder Guards

Being a healer is never an easy job. Standing right in the mix of things can make even the most balanced spirit feel a bit chaotic. Once worn by Jurond the Steadfast, these shoulder guards exemplify his strength of spirit, to stand fast in the face of adversity and triumph. "May they give you strength when you feel weak," is still etched into the underside of the leather.

+3 Strength +3 Intelligence +4 Wisdom +1 to all secondary stats.

Tim equipped his new shoulder guards and shrugged a few times to get used to the additional weight. His strength was at twenty finally, and he felt slightly different. Hitting the first milestone must've given him a decent boost. Gone were the days of asking ShadowLily to carry his heavy things.

Or maybe not. It was kind of nice not being the group's pack mule.

The chest disappeared in a beautiful swirl of golden motes, and someone banged on the gate behind them.

"Guess we should probably let them in." Cassie ran toward the gate and lifted the massive beam holding it closed.

Commander Valiant walked through the archway with a hundred men at her back. She looked at the crater in the street and back at her men. "Send word we need dirt and someone to repair the cobbles."

Turning her attention away from the destruction, Valiant focused on Tim. "The king has sent word. You are expected at the castle immediately."

Tim didn't want to start another fight, but he wasn't about to go to the castle when they were so close to saving his friends. "We can't go until we stop the wedding."

Shaking her head, Commander Valiant motioned behind her, and a carriage pulled forward bearing the royal crest. "That's what the king wants to talk to you about. Something is blocking the entrance to the duke's castle, and he needs your help."

There wasn't any getting out of this without taking on the whole damn army. "Send word to the king that we'd be delighted."

Turning back to his party, Tim pointed at the carriage. "The king is going to help us get inside the duke's castle."

Cassie trudged past him toward the carriage, looking tired. "Do you think Brother Khalil has any of those little cakes lying around?"

"I'm sure the king will have someone make us something to eat and give us a place to get cleaned up." JaKobi slipped into the carriage with Lorelei right on his heels.

ShadowLily stopped next to Tim and kissed him. "I don't like the thought of leaving our friends with the duke any longer than we have to."

"I know what you mean." Tim kissed her this time. "I'll shoot a quick message to Liz so she doesn't worry, and one to Prince Desmond about the currency of our situation."

He followed ShadowLily into the carriage. Right when he thought all they had left to do was face the duke, it turned out their adventure was only the beginning.

LIST OF TIM'S CURRENT STATS AND SKILLS

"Tim" level twenty-two Hex Witch
Primary Stats
Strength: 20
Endurance: 44
Dexterity: 32
Intelligence: 67
Wisdom: 82
Perception: 6
Vitality: 4
Revitalization: 4
Luck: 7

Notable Gear
Weapons
Simple Dagger of Dexterity, +1 (X2)
Greater Staff of Yin, +3 Endurance +7 Intelligence +7 Wisdom
Shiri's Orb of Greater Healing, +5 Endurance +5 Intelligence +7 Wisdom, Special ability: Serve the Needy

LIST OF TIM'S CURRENT STATS AND SKILLS

Armor

Eye of Krathos, +3 Endurance +5 Intelligence +7 Wisdom

Hex Witch's Shoulder Guards, +3 Strength +3 Intelligence +4 Wisdom +1 to all secondary stats

Hex Witch's Armament, +2 Endurance +2 Dexterity +6 Intelligence +8 Wisdom

Dragon Hyde Jerkin, +2 to all base stats, +1 to all secondary stats

Bearhide Wrist Guards of the Faithful, +1 Endurance +1 Wisdom, Special ability: Bear Necessities

Paul's Gloves of Mending, +7 Intelligence +4 Wisdom

Vindicator's Belt of Healing, +2 Endurance +3 Intelligence +5 Wisdom

No That's Not a Brown Spot Leather Pants, +3 Endurance +2 Dexterity +4 Intelligence +3 Wisdom, Special ability: Flee

Arlen's Boots of Chaotic Intent, +3 Endurance +4 Intelligence +6 Wisdom, Special ability: Chaotic Intent any skills effectiveness will be increased or decreased by one to ten percent.

Jewelry and Accessories

Arlen's Bracelet of Balance, +2 Endurance +4 Dexterity, Special ability: influence the outcome of Chaotic Intent

Band of Retention, +3 Endurance +2 Dexterity, Special ability: mana feedback

Ring of Luminosity, +1 Endurance +2 Intelligence +3 Wisdom

Necklace of Hydration, +1 Endurance +2 Intelligence +5 Wisdom

Trinket of the Smiling Monkey, +1 to a random stat

Skills

Appeal to the Goddess: Apprentice rank one

Curse of Sacrifice: Apprentice rank one

LIST OF TIM'S CURRENT STATS AND SKILLS

Hex of the Shattered Beast: Apprentice rank one
Night Vision: Apprentice rank four
Backstab: Apprentice rank five
Throwing Knives: Apprentice rank five
Shadow Master: Apprentice rank six
Sneak: Apprentice rank six
Disturbance: Apprentice rank nine
Rectify: Apprentice rank nine
Quick Feet: Journeyman rank one
Small Blades: Journeyman rank one
Snare: Journeyman rank four
Flame Burst: Journeyman rank eight
Dodge: Journeyman rank nine
Healing Storm: Journeyman rank nine
Behold My Power: Master rank one
Divine Light: Master rank one
Who Needs a Shield: Master rank one
Cleanse: Master rank two
Curse of Giving: Master rank two
Healing Orb: Master rank six

Stances
Way of the River
Way of the Boulder

Buffs
Weaken Undead: Journeyman rank five
Armor of Eternia: Journeyman rank nine
Attacks of the Faithful: Journeyman rank nine

Open Quests
The Stone of Immoratis

THE STORY CONTINUES

The story continues with book fourteen, *Ravenstorm's Last Dance*, coming soon to Amazon and Kindle Unlimited.

OTHER BOOKS BY BRADFORD BATES

The Helsing Society
(with Michael Anderle)
One Step Past Sundown (Book 1)
Past Bites (Book 2)
Ashes of the Fallen (Book 3)
Fate of the West (Book 4)

Rise Of The Grandmaster Series
(with Michael Anderle)
Rise of the Grandmaster (Book 1)
The Trials of Tristholm (Book 2)
Deserts Of Naroosh (Book 3)
The Eyes of Prophecy (Book 4)
Battle for the Kingdom (Book 5)

Ascendancy Legacy
The Arena
Jar of Souls
Guardian of the Grove
Demon Stone
The Rising Darkness
Redemption

Ascendancy Origins
Rise of the Fallen
Butcher of the Bay

Night of the Demon

The Bozley Green Chronicles
Possessed

The Galactic Outlaws
Forced Compliance

Genetic Purge

Smuggler's Legacy

Fortune Hunters
Star Talon

Lost Signal

A Galactic Outlaws Story
The Marchenko Incident

Smuggler for Hire

Origin Ice

The Fairy of Salem
Witching Hour

The Wild Hunt

Standalone Titles
Crimson Stars

BOOKS BY MICHAEL ANDERLE

Sign up for the LMBPN email list to be notified of new releases and special deals!

https://lmbpn.com/email/

For a complete list of books by Michael Anderle, please visit:

www.lmbpn.com/ma-books/

CONNECT WITH THE AUTHORS

Connect with Bradford Bates

Facebook:
https://www.facebook.com/bradfordbatesauthor/

Twitter:
https://twitter.com/Freetheblizz

Website:
http://www.bradfordbates.com/

Connect with Michael Anderle

Website: http://lmbpn.com

Email List: http://lmbpn.com/email/

https://www.facebook.com/LMBPNPublishing

https://twitter.com/MichaelAnderle

https://www.instagram.com/lmbpn_publishing/

https://www.bookbub.com/authors/michael-anderle

ABOUT BRADFORD BATES

Bradford Bates is a full-time author, husband to an incredible wife, and father to four furry rescue dogs. He lives in sunny Phoenix, Arizona, trying to not melt in the oppressive heat of the summer. When he isn't busy writing the next book, you can find him playing video games and watching scary movies.

www.ingramcontent.com/pod-product-compliance
Lightning Source LLC
LaVergne TN
LVHW041946070526
838199LV00051BA/2924